TIME BOMB'S DREAM

M.K. Rylynn

Cover design by M.K. Rylynn

Edited by Cyrus Literary Productions

First Edition

ISBN: 979-8-218-74167-9

Printed in the United States of America

Contact: m.k.books333@gmail.com

Rampage

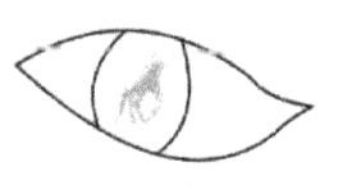

Nightmare

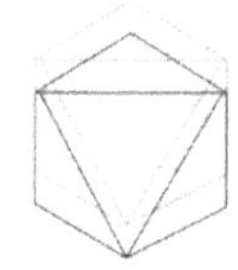

Rogue

Nexus

Phantom

Contents

Chapter 1

Their lungs wheeze as *it* creeps closer, Humid, slimy, slivering down trachea and airways with each shaky inhale.

This can't be all we are here for? To die?

Likely.

Emerald bites at the horizon, its dense fog blurring their recollections; every path appears the same.

"Ophelia." His sharp voice tings, the crouching form in front of the door barring his dizzy glare. "You think you could go any faster? I thought you were good at picking locks."

"This would be so much easier if I didn't have the *village idiot* breathing down my neck, watching my every move." The woman grumbles, she's lost count of how many times Chase risked their lives to demand back control. She nudges each pin upward — a *click* ringing amongst their shallow breaths. See? Just a few more...

Chase growls, coughing as he reaches to grab her shoulders. The air pulses between them, Nicholas's green sparks appearing just in time. A glaring human barricade, he shoves his older brother back. "Don't... You'll screw up the last chance we have to complete —" he hisses, a sharp pain in his chest startling his focus.

Ophelia swallows her frustration, her clenched fist dropping as Nicholas gasps. Her own head throbs in tune with his tremors. She hurries back to the door. She doesn't have time, they don't have time, but this pin refuses to give in! She glances at Nicholas again, stepping back with a determined grimace.

"This is gonna hurt." She raises her hands, with controlled breath, she summons the cold, and ice shoots at the large padlock. Stumbling at the surge, she gestures weakly at Chase. "Kick... it..."

An iron taste fills Nicholas' gums, his hand clasping over his mouth as a cough bursts through. Crimson drips from his fingers, a thin line trailing down the corner of his mouth.

His eyes widen at the scarlet on his palm. Fresh blood. His blood.

"Dammit! He is trying to get rid of us. Karmin! Casey! Ellis!" He slurs, making his way over to the frozen door and gesturing for Ophelia's arm with his unmarked hand. "We have to go. This is a trap! This air isn't just drugged, it's filled with poison! We're all going to die if we spend any more time here!"

Three more kids emerge through the doorways of the building's cramped interior, their shoulders slumped, moving sluggishly.

Casey sways on his feet, rubbing one tired eye with the heel of his hand — a deep yawn splitting his sentence before he can get any words out.

Karmin drags her sleeve across her mouth, heterochromatic eyes narrowing as she scans the fog-choked room. "We can't find anything dad would want us to destroy —" Karmin hacks, quieting as the words hit her.

Ellis taps the doorframe with two fingers, head tilted. "What's this about dad trying to kill us?" He frowns, the leisure lift to his tone meeting silence, and an eye roll from Chase.

"What are you talking about *Rogue*? We've been ordered to destroy any tech we see. We haven't finished. We still need to get behind this door —!" Chase chokes out the codename, knowing how it aggravates his brother. This mission has a reason, a *real* reason, and therefore a real villain; and it can't be their father. Ophelia *struggles* to open the lock. It shouldn't take her this long to open the door. Surely her *talents* work better than this.

"This is a death trap Chase! How can you not see that, really! You of all people, should be the one making this call!" He shouts back with a glare, quietly grateful that Preston's wife had taken pity and given them all names, otherwise he'd never be rid of *that*.

Ophelia wilts at the sight of his bloodied hand, meeting his wide eyes with her own. Why would his father send his own kids to die? She obviously doesn't know Preston as well as the others, but surely that can't be it. Right?

Chase breaks her thoughts as his ranting grows into a gurgle. They need to get out of here. The fog consumes the room, leaving little space untouched, but it has to have a point of origin. Her eyes dart down to the bottom of the door. The mist could be going under it just as much as it could be coming from it, but no other way makes sense!

"Chase, this crap has to be coming from behind the door." She rasps, leaning against Nicholas. "If we open it, it'll kill us faster." She looks down the long hallway they came from. They wouldn't make it back in time before the gas takes over completely.

Nicholas nods, swatting at the mist. "She's right, we open that door, and we are dead. *That's* the whole purpose of this mission." His complexion drains, his stomach churns, he pays it no mind.

Ophelia straightens her posture, facing the others. "I can teleport us out of here, it'll just be to the outside of the building, but that should be enough to get you away from the poison."

Karmin's brow raises. "Are you sure you'll be able to get us all out of here? I can barely use my powers. I don't know how much energy you'll use trying to get us out."

"We don't have much of a choice. We can't go back the way we came, and we certainly will not be opening that door." She steps and takes Karmin's hand, gesturing for Casey to hold onto Ellis. "I'll take you guys in groups." She disappears in a flash of purple light.

"Karmin is right, I'll make a portal and—" Before he can finish, another pulse of lavender flares, Ophelia already grabbing the others to evacuate. His jaw pinches. He knows what this does to her, her actions are counterproductive in his eyes.

He turns around to Chase who still tries to breach the door. "You're done now." His voice manages to stay assertive despite its growing weakness.

"I'm not going," Chase coughs, stepping back. "If we leave now, it'll be a failed mission. I am not going back to Dad after failing a mission."

Ophelia appears, her eyes shut as she tries to keep the energy of her power from faltering. If Chase wants to waste his breath, it gives her a moment to recuperate — The image of the blood spouting from Nicholas's mouth keeps her untethered, she needs to get them out of there.

Nicholas balls his fists, pale green light soon emitting from his shaky hands as a portal opens a few paces away. Blood pours from his throat in clumps; the portal weaker than needed. "Hurry! It's going to collapse if you don't leave right now!"

With a grunt he delivers another surge of energy forwards. "Chase, now is not the time for your psychological issues. Jump through the damn portal before I bring it to you—" He snaps back over to Ophelia "You need to go back with the others, get yourself out while you can! I'll take care of Chase and meet you on the other side—" Pain racks through his body "—Use my portal, Ophelia. Please!"

Her eyes prod open. It pains her to see him this way, looking seconds from death; he always makes sure to get everyone out.

Watching him struggle to hold the portal makes her blood freeze, and she curses him for being so stubborn. Chase kills their chances the longer they stay here. “Nicholas, please. Let me.” She raises her palms again.

“No. You’ll overwork yourself and then you’ll be as useful as Chase.” He spits out angrily.

Ophelia’s eyes narrow, making a grab for Chase’s arm and yanking him back from the door. He stumbles, his enhanced strength out of commission from the poison.

“You’re giving me so many reasons—” forcing him to the portal “—To leave your ass here.”

She shoves him through the portal before he can protest, the door behind them rattling from the pressure on the other end.

"Shit. Come on!" She hurries, grabbing a hold of Nicholas too and dragging him to his own portal. "I don't trust you to follow me out."

Ophelia steps back as it closes completely, sucking him in before collapsing, leaving her on the other side. She draws what little energy she can muster to teleport, a booming crack averting her attention. "Crap—"

The mist comes rushing untethered and at full force.

Nicholas lands upon the pavement on his side, groaning. He abruptly pushes himself to stand, nearly tumbling over. Eyes wide with panic, he tries to crawl towards the building. Hands balled as he demands the portal back, but nothing comes.

The poison has drained his powers significantly. He shrieks, managing to a standing position as he paces the ground, wiping his bloodied mouth on his sleeve.

Chase watches the building as vapors leak from its bolted windows. Shaking his head and scoffing, he plops himself down on a bus bench. “Serves her right.”

Nicholas whirls around and stares at him with wild, manic eyes.

“What? She probably caused it anyway. I don’t trust her.”

If he had anything in his hands, he’d throw it. A nearby pebble smiles up at him. It goes flying and hits Chase's temple head-on. "Shut up! You would have died if it wasn't for her."

Preparing to reach for another rock — a purple light catches his peripherals. His gut jumps with hope, and with what little energy he has left, he sprints in its direction.

He manages to catch her as she passes out, her whisper barely making it through his haze of concern. Nicholas sinks to his knees, scanning over her before taking her more comfortably in his arms.

His head lifts in a scowl as his siblings' gaze raises his alarm. "Am I not allowed to have a moment?" He stands up slowly, sure not to jostle her. He won't be able to carry her all the way back to his house. His lungs taking no more than the acceptable moment to reprieve, he brings himself to teleport them directly to his room.

Ellis stares at where his brother stood, “Well, it looks like we are walking back.”

The other three grumble angrily, tired as they make their way back to the house.

Ophelia’s warning remains in the air, unheard by their sluggish minds.

She’s coming.

Chapter 2

Ophelia's eyes shot open. She lay on a black couch in what looked like an office — the white tiles impulsively clean, unlike those of the building she passed out in.

The black leather couch beneath her sat pushed against a wall, the only wrinkles formed where she sat, the rest in pristine condition. Too perfect. A desk of dark wood rests in the center of the room. An immaculate surface with nothing upon it. No pens. No papers. No staplers.

The accompanying high-back office chair seems more like a throne than a piece of furniture, with faint scratches marring the leather.

The space held an absence of the personal; no photos, no mementos, only an unnerving emptiness. The stark and deliberate lighting leaves corners of the room cast in shadow. The darkness moved, then spoke. *"Relax Time Bomb."*

A woman slipped into the light, taking her seat at the desk, movements measured and voice soft.

Short, platinum white hair, framed her face, barring a single streak of black hair. Her pale gray eyes, sharp and calculating, pierced through Ophelia. While otherwise calm and serene, her smile held the faintest edge; her gaze lingering a fraction too long.

"I have an offer for you..."

Chapter 3

Staggering to his bed Nicholas lays Ophelia down. He takes a moment to catch his breath in the clean air. He doesn't feel as horrid as he did before, but the poison lingers still. Ophelia must be feeling it too.

As he stands assessing what to do, a muffled shout comes from downstairs in the main room of the house.

"You know the rules, Preston. Ophelia is my daughter and any mission you want with my children must come through me first! Where is she?" Thomas O'Connor's voice carries through the hallway. The usually soft spoken man paces, the danger Preston Peters imposed on his daughter leaving no room for pleasantries.

“I do not know. They left hours ago and have not yet returned” He speaks simply, “I fear they might not have been as equipped to handle it. Though I am not surprised due to their lack of care during their training.”

“Of course, you do not care about your own children. You treat them as lab rats!” His voice grows louder as he ascends the stairs to Nicholas’ room. “You do not get to treat my Ophelia this way!”

“They are not *normal* children.” Preston replies, storming up after him.

Nicholas can hear them in the hallway, hoping they opt on venturing into his room. He wants to spend time with Ophelia, even if she was unconscious. Hearing her heartbeat brings him comfort, makes it easier to forgive her stubbornness.

The door to the bedroom opens, Thomas taking notice of his daughter upon his bed. "What happened to her?" He pushes into the room. "I need to know *exactly* what happened."

Nicholas eyes the two men carefully, unhinged with a feigned composure. "There was some sort of poison exposure during our mission. She breathed quite a bit into her system, and she pushed her limits—" He gestures to her prone form "—This is the product of over-exertion and poor planning."

Thomas gently scoops the girl into his arms "I need to take her home. I knew her hanging around here would be bad for her. Preston cares for no one but himself," he mumbles to the boy, knowing he and his daughter were close, his anger not directed towards them. He refuses to allow Preston's careless behavior towards his own kids to rub off on Ophelia.

Nicholas slowly steps back, his eyes still scanning the situation as it plays out. "Have room for one more? I am not letting her out of my sight. Not until I know she's alive and functioning."

The older man sighs. "I suppose you could join me." He starts for the door, glaring at Preston.

"Wait—" Nicholas pauses, the memory coming back to him as his adrenaline calms "—Before she passed out, she delivered a strange message: *She's coming*." He takes a step closer to Thomas, cocking his head to the side. "Have any idea what she might be referring to?"

Preston has the proper means and intentions, but he can't trust Thomas too quickly. Not with the evident planning behind this sabotage.

That trade belonged to Thomas, easily. Could he have been waiting for them to come back weak, or even not at all? He follows him down the stairs to the front door, his car waiting outside, ignition still on.

"She's coming?" He murmurs softly, lips pressed in a line as he thinks, "I'm afraid I have no clue... I know you have been trained to be skeptical of everything, but I assure you I am on your side. Ophelia left this morning without telling me. I came here after she hadn't returned. It's not like her to hide from me where she's going."

Not yet convinced, he welcomes himself to the passenger seat. He grew up learning to adhere to his own morals and judgement over any authority figure, and that includes even Thomas. "I am still coming with her, I will not leave her side." His eyes fall on Ophelia's relaxed face. "Besides, whatever poison she has, I have too. We need an antidote."

Thomas lays her in the back, climbing into the driver's seat waiting for Nicholas to get situated before driving. "I don't have an antidote—" he says glancing at him "—I have an ice chamber used to keep Ophelia regulated. If she gets too hot, the ice in her system acts funny, I doubt it'll be able to help with the poison, but it could slow down anything that might happen to her."

After a moment, the older man turns to face him directly. "Were your siblings there? Where are they now? It shouldn't be too hard for me to work on an antidote."

Nicholas leans against the door, eyes on the rolling scenery from the window. "I'm not their keeper. But they *were* with us at the mission site.

Ophelia saved them, pushing her limits and draining her strength to do it." He scoffs "I specifically told her not to. But no one ever listens to me." He looks over at Ophelia, eyes conveying something unable to be put into words. "I could come up with some kind of antidote. I just need lab equipment; I can run some tests based off the poison in my own system."

They arrive at the house, Thomas taking Ophelia inside and making his way to the basement. Seven other children try and peer over his shoulder, though his focus stays on the girl in his arms. Past a hallway, a room containing a large metal chamber emerges. The chamber has a thick reinforced door, and small, rectangular windows with wire mesh embedded in the glass. Mounted upon the adjacent wall rests a red button.

Laying Ophelia on the chamber's bed, he presses the red button, its gears groaning loudly as the door shuts with a thud. Adjusting the dials upon the panel before the chamber, the windows begin to freeze over.

"Alright, if it pleases you, you can stay down here and keep an eye on her." He gestures to a chair he can rest in. "I will go see what I can do about the poison. You rest here."

Nicholas watches the process curiously wanting to know how it works — but more pressing matters exist.

Keeping Ophelia safe.

Get this poison out of his own system.

Determine if Thomas can be trusted.

His eyes flicker towards the other man, an unsettling grin pulling at his lips. "I think I'll stay."

"Very well, I will go figure out a remedy." He makes his way to the exit, scowling. "Unlike Preston, I care for my children."

The door slams behind him. Only once Thomas leaves does he allow himself to pry his gaze from the door. He heads back to Ophelia, standing in front of the window with his head tilted towards the device. Studying it.

He clenches his jaw. "Yeah, this doesn't look like it's going well for us, does it? Maybe if you just listened to me instead of trying to play hero." His green eyes scan her features, his worry overriding his frustration with her. "I'll fix this. I'll be sure of it. Then you can tell me what you mean by 'she's coming'"

A door opening and the clicking of heels silences his one-sided conversation. A dark-haired woman wearing a blue dress walked towards the chamber, not acknowledging Nicholas, a dark-haired girl accompanying her side. Her small gaze fixed on Nicholas.

The woman looks down at the girl before noticing Nicholas. “Oh, you must be that boy Ophelia always speaks of.” She turns back to the glass, but the kid’s eyes never leave his face. She looks as though staring into his soul, her hands clasped in front of her, unblinking.

Frustration bubbles up inside of him, he just wants one single moment to think! He rolls his eyes slightly, only to be caught off guard by the third last word. “Always?” He repeats quietly to himself. The short-lived confusion disappears as the kid continues to stare at him, his defensive instincts kicking in.

"He thinks it's Preston's doing. He is frustrated that Ophelia didn't listen... and he doesn't trust us." She beams, tilting her head as she rattles off.

Nicholas swats a hand in front of her face. "Hey! That's none of your damn business, stay out of my mind!"

The girl just grins, the woman stepping behind them and scolding her. "Alice. What have I told you about reading people's minds without permission?"

"But they're screaming at me..." The kid whines.

The woman waves her daughters' words away, focusing back on Nicholas. "Yes, always. She speaks of nothing but you, and someone named Ellis."

He scrunches up his face. "Ellis?" Ellis being on the same level as him in Ophelia's mind baffles him. He shakes his head, growing frustrated at the distractions. "Don't you all have something better to do than bother me? Ophelia isn't going to like being stared at by all of you when she wakes up."

The woman looks down at Nicholas. "I am not bothering you. I came here to watch over my daughter." It's clear she does not like his tone, nor how he tries to gain control of the room. She turns back to look at Ophelia, her gaze softening. "She hates being in this thing."

"Don't pay attention to him, Mom," Alice starts, "I think he just wants to be alone to confess his love to Ophelia..." Growing bored, her mother scolds her again and sends her out.

Nicholas' limbs grow heavy. The adrenaline leaving him completely. He pulls over the chair, keeping his eyes on Ophelia. "Got any coffee around here?"

The woman perks at the request. "...Yes, I just put on a fresh pot. I'll be back." She turns and leaves.

The moment the door shuts, Ophelia's eyes shoot open. Her breathing slow, not yet registering what happened. All at once, she bolts up, hyperventilating. The adrenaline blends further with the poison already in her system, and she passes out once more.

"Ophelia- stay with me!" He rushes towards the chamber, restraining himself from forcing his way in and shaking her shoulders. He tugs on his hair, kicking the wall. It feels good in the moment, but pain soon tingles up his leg. A slew of curse words flow from his mouth.

The door opens again, heels echoing across the floor. “Did she wake up?” Ophelia’s mother takes in his agitated scowl, setting a tray of food and coffee on a nearby table, making her way to her daughter. “Should I go get Thomas?”

He turns to the woman slowly, his eye twitching. “Oh, you mean you couldn’t hear her yelling from upstairs? She woke up for two seconds and then passed back out.” He spits out, walking towards the door. “Where is your lab?”

Her haze narrows, the kitchen nowhere near this *soundproof* room. “Through the hallway to the right. If you reach the carpeted stairs, you’ve gone too far,” she says, handing him a cup of coffee and exiting swiftly with her tray.

He watches her leave, cursing himself. The longest interaction with Ophelia's parents, and he'd been too stressed to make a decent impression.

Coffee in hand, he follows the directions easily. Chugging the cup's contents, his energy begins to return. He will discover this cure. Him. Not Thomas.

Once he gets to the lab, he sees Thomas tinkering with various cylinders of liquid, working alongside one of his sons, Ollie and his other daughter Iris —in case he needs a plant-based cure.

"Ollie, my journal is on my shelf over there. I can't remember which item is next," He says, gesturing to the two vials, "I must put them in the correct order, otherwise this will explode."

Oliver simply nods before levitating off the ground grabbing the red journal for his father. He watches in the air as Thomas flips through the pages.

"Here." Thomas murmurs, pouring the vial on the right first and then adding the last one. The mixture turns dark blue. "It's done, Iris can you go grab the boy that's downstairs? He came home with Ophelia and offered— more like demanded that the cure be tested on him."

"Search no further," Nicholas said, opting to keep his mouth shut about the possible explosion. "The test subject—" he scans the strange chemical concoction, "— Has arrived." A coy smile on his face, his demeanor changes completely, happy to have a remedy ready for testing.

"So how does this work, O'Connor? Injection? Ingestion? Inhalation?"

Thomas's brow lifts at the approach, the lack of snarky or witty comments surprising him

"Right." He picks up the bottle of blue liquid "Ingestion. I try to stay away from needles due to Ophelia's fear of them. She makes her skin so cold that the needles break on impact." He smiles fondly, handing over the bottle.

Nicholas takes the vile and throws his head back, not allowing a single drop to stick around on his tongue. No instant relief, but it does settle fairly quickly, the once crushing pain in his lungs calming. Impressive.

Thomas starts to clean up his desk. "How is she doing? Was she awake before you left?" He glances at the clock, thirty minutes passing since he left her down there. The time had not settled the anger in him that wanted to kick Preston's ass for what he had done to his daughter.

Their only commonality is their adoption of superpowered children. Both men hold guardianship of different powered children, expected to provide care and schooling for those with nowhere else to go; parental death, being abandoned or kicked out, some didn't even truly know their origins.

A strong part of Thomas wanted to keep Ophelia away from Preston's kids, but Ophelia came home one day, rambling about making a powered friend. Despite his concern, her happiness always took precedence.

"She did," Nicholas says with a nod. "But she passed out again." He smirks as he sets the vial down on the counter and sticks his finger in the air as if he were at a bar asking for another drink. "One more drink for the lady, please."

"I figured that would be the case," he says, waving his hand around. "Poison threw her system out of balance, and it will only continue that way if we can't remove it." His voice falters, his eyes distant for a moment. "I am quite curious about the mission you went on. Preston assigned it to you, I'm assuming. What exactly was the task?"

Nicholas raises his eyebrow. "I'm afraid that information isn't available to disclose with the nonaffiliated." He keeps his eyes on the liquid solution as Thomas transfers it to another vial.

"I'll make some for your siblings, my son, Tyler, will run them to you when they're done." He hands him the vial. "Try to be gentle with her once she comes to. I don't want to risk her becoming overwhelmed."

Nicholas takes the vial and grins. "I'm always careful" With that, he teleports out of that room. The chamber stands as cold as he left it, Ophelia still unconscious inside. The giant door unlocks with a smack to the button; he only enters once warmth meets his skin. He can't afford getting frost bite right now.

He stands in front of her, still smiling, proud that he will be the one to provide her with the cure for the toxins in her system. Hopefully, there won't be any more interruptions. That way they can be alone... and she can explain what she meant.

He gently lifts her head, holding the vial to her lips. Careful as not to make her choke, he pours the fluid at a slow pace.

Dark marks distort the light blue hue of her skin, her powers blending with the poison. After a moment, the black fades from her pores. Movement shifts beneath her eyelids.

"Tastes... awful."

Ophelia's eyes peek open, her voice soft yet raspy. She opens her eyes and speaks softly. "Now, before you yell at me, just know—I would much rather you didn't. I'll take a hug, though?"

His smile grows into a wide grin, his shoulders easing at the sight of her awakening. Realizing she can see him, he flattens immediately, though secretly grateful to have her still around. "I'm not going to yell at you in your home. You get a free pass because you've been out for the last hour and a half. But don't give me reasons to revoke your privileges."

He allows the corner of his mouth to rise into a short-lived side-grin. Though, the second request made him falter. Nicholas' lack of outward affection makes for some great jokes, fun-packed stories where he chases her for messing up his hair. Normally, he shoots down such an ask — the possibility of her messing with him, fearing embarrassment, or worse, the exposure of his true feelings far too risky. Yet...

A sigh leaves his lips. "Yeah. Sure, whatever. Have at it." He couldn't be caught dead exposed like this, offering himself to the girl for a hug. Yet here he stands, arms held out in surrender, waiting for her touch.

"Awe, how sweet, thanks for the pass." She pokes his nose gently, taking notice of the light grin he had let slip. She carefully sits up, swinging her legs to the side, looking around while trying to come to.

Not wanting to ruin her chance, she tries to contain her excitement. Sliding off the bed and hugging him close to her, her arms gently wrap around his shoulders, her face pressing into his neck. She relaxes leaning against him. She needed this. To be held. To be held without feeling the annoyance from the other person. Her fingers carefully make their way to the back of his head, gently playing with his hair. Nicholas's arms lower as she goes for his shoulders, stiffening at first contact but ultimately relaxing into her embrace. Her hand combing through his hair proves to be surprisingly comforting. With her face buried in his neck, he can't help the blush in his complexion, glad she can't see it.

Silence falls between them as they stand. Nicholas takes a step forward, hiding his face in her shoulder as his arms reciprocate, snaking around her waist; pulling her closer to him, pressed to one another in place. Heat radiates from his skin, his powers using his body much like an electrical generator.

Sweet Ophelia O'Connor gets along with everyone — well, most people. She had a better childhood than most, especially compared to how Preston treats Nicholas. Though, the voices still creep into her mind, telling her how annoying others find her. Growing up she learned quickly which of her family members could handle her bubbly personality, and which ones would subtly scold her for it.

When first meeting Nicholas, Ophelia assumed he would be the latter, but here he was, undeniably stressed from the mission, having every right to be angry with the cards dealt to him, and he holds her. He could've rolled his eyes and left once she felt better, scolding her for being reckless. He could've given her a weak one-armed hug and called it good. But he stands here. Supporting her.

She feels his arms pull her closer, and she could just melt right here and now, turning to putty in the boy's gentle touch. The inviting heat coils from him, a comforting presence that never overwhelms. She feels *safe*.

"Alright, I think that's my record time for hugs." He breathes out, stepping back from the interaction, his hands back in their pockets. Eying her cautiously, as if nothing happened, but the blush on his face calls him a liar. “Earlier, before you blacked out, you said someone was coming. Who is this ‘she’? Do you remember?”

Ophelia pulls away, smiling playfully at how quickly he moves to business talk. “Nicholas, let’s get out of the ice chamber, yeah? You’ll catch a cold.”

She takes his arm and walks out of the metal door, heading towards the panel to turn the machine off entirely. His words catch up to her. “I said that someone was coming?” She raises her eyebrow, trying to think of everything that happened. She remembers being hit with mist, and then directly after, waking up in the chamber.

Nicholas stares at the spot on his arm which she guides him from. Used to being ignored, his body’s natural reactions to the cold, quiet. “I’m not going to catch a cold, my immune system is superior to the average human. Try me."

His eyes narrow at her recollection, or in better terms, lack thereof. If she can't remember, then how can they prepare? "How do you not remember? You said she was coming, you're telling me that doesn't ring a bell?" He tilts his head. "Listen, you're the one who stayed behind. You are the only eyewitness we have available."

"I don't know how I don't remember Nicholas, I literally have no idea what you're talking about" She shakes her head. "Maybe you imagined it? I'm pretty sure lack of sleep and poison creates hallucinations." Ophelia tries, though her voice lacks serenity.

"Well —" His voice is barely above a whisper. "You could be right, I suppose." Nicholas shrugs off his anxieties projecting his voice to reassert his confidence. “The real test would be to see if the others remember as much.” He pauses remembering the remedies Thomas had promised his siblings. “You’re coming with me.” Taking her wrist, he leads her back upstairs to the main room. “We have to make a delivery, and we need everyone with us to discuss the mission.”

“There you are,” A voice calls from the couch. Ophelia’s brother, Tyler stands up, lifting up the briefcase previously resting against the couch. He hands it to Nicholas with a raised eyebrow. “You’re not leaving with her, now are you?” He stands a bit straighter, clearly protective of his sister, especially after *this*. “I’m pretty sure our father would rather have her stay here where she is *safe*.”

Nicholas does not appreciate Tyler's tone, regardless of if he expects it. "I think she can make her own decisions, without her father's input." The words leave him faster than he can stop them, and he glances over at Ophelia for her statement in the matter.

"I'll be fine, Tyler. I'll take it easy, and I'll come back at the first sign of trouble, or aggression from Preston." She promises.

Her voice seems to soften his stance, Tyler nods without meeting her eye, walking off.

Chapter 4

Thomas stands just outside the cold chamber, the soft hum of the cooling system a cruel reminder of what this means. His fingers linger on the thick glass, tracing invisible lines as if trying to connect with his daughter trapped inside. The room's walls are soundproof, but he knows why. Every muffled cry, every sharp intake of breath would tear through him like a blade.

His jaw clenches, but he doesn't let himself look away from the sealed door. He swallows hard, the tase of regret bitter on his tongue. The faintest tremor runs through his hands, but he keeps them steady, pushing down the urge to open the door, to reach through the barrier and pull her out.

He tells himself this is for her own good. If he lets the sound reach him, if he lets his walls break, it'll be worse for both of them.

His eyes flicker to Ophelia. The quiet screams inside are hers alone to bear, and the silence outside is his penance.

Chapter 5

When the two appear in Preston's home, only two of the boys are there.

"Oh, look who finally decided to show up," Casey mumbles tiredly, looking at Nicholas through the brown hair that falls over his eyes— far too exhausted to properly style it.

Ellis gasps standing wobbly, like a toddler learning how to take his first steps. "You're alive!" He throws his arms around Ophelia. "Guys, she's not dead!"

Nicholas rolls his eyes at both comments, taking the antidotes out of the case and placing them onto the table. "Just call the rest of the family down, everyone needs to take this antidote before the poison can cause any more damage."

"Nicholas is here!" Ellis yells in a singsong voice to the others upstairs. He grabs a vial and downs it quickly, shrugging afterwards. "Not the worst thing I've taken." He flops down on the couch, pulling Ophelia down with him. "You're staying by my side. Mkay?"

Nicholas watches the two on the couch, somewhat uncomfortable with the sight, but unable to figure out why. He pulls his gaze away, scanning the room for anything else to keep his focus on. Karmin and Chase descended the stairs shortly after, the effects of their swallowed antidotes taking effect alongside their siblings'.

Finally feeling better, Chase wastes no time moving to stand before Ophelia. "So, who is it?" He glares down at her. "Who is it that you are working for?"

"Chase, stop. She is not working with anyone. She is one of us, there is no betrayal here." Nicholas sighs annoyed. "If there was, I would have detected it long before you."

"I really don't know who you're talking about," Ophelia starts, "Chase, my father adopted me for the same reason yours did."

He shakes his head. "No. You were talking about some lady, and I can only assume that you were telling us the truth because you felt guilty and wanted us to know before you died." He gets closer to her face. "I will not hesitate to get the truth out of you."

Ophelia stays still, glaring up at him. "Back. Off."

"Chase, your breath smells really bad—" Ellis whispers, hoping to defuse the tension a bit.

"Chase, that's enough. Lay a hand on her and you'll lose it. Got it?" Could he actually uphold that promise in his current recovering condition, no. Would he try anyway? Absolutely.

Chase gives Ellis a death glare, before addressing Nicholas directly while his gaze returns to Ophelia. "You know, you wouldn't have been able to detect anything, because you're not focused. Just like Dad said, on the rare occasions that our families have joint missions, you get sloppy. Give it up, Ophelia. You're just trying to take us down from the inside. It won't work, but what it will do is get Nicholas killed. Is that what you want to happen?"

Everyone had been there for last month's yelling match. *How could he have let himself be so distracted that he had to be saved by her?*

Venom-like anger fills his face. “Sloppy?” He scoffs. “I’m sorry, who brought you the antidote? Your lungs would be filled with blood right now.”

He could totally take him. “Yeah, the antidote you got from *Thomas O’Connor?* Our father’s enemy? Real smart move, Nicholas. We could all be dead in a matter of minutes.”

Ellis’s shoulders lift in horror, eyes wide. “I can see all of you guys.” He holds his hands in front of his face, hesitant and shaky.

Karmin puts a reassuring hand on his shoulder, bright eyes watching the scene hesitantly.

“Why do you care so much?” Chase spits back.

“Care?” He hisses. “What, is that something I am incapable of doing now? Aren’t I allowed to have a friend or two? Jesus, Chase. Not everything falls under the simplicity of black and white. Ophelia is my friend, and she saved my life." He keeps his eyes on him. "She saved yours too. I would be a bit more appreciative."

"Careful, Nicholas, if you friend-zone her, that might cause her to snap." The older brother looks back at Ophelia "Is that the only reason you haven't attacked us yet? What are you waiting for? Who's orders?"

Chase's proximity to her face makes Ophelia overwhelmed, and she teleports to create a space between them, landing a few paces behind him.

He reacts on pure, unthinking instinct.

His fist lashes out before he registers his actions, fearing her motion. The punch connects, the impact sending Ophelia hurtling into the wall with a thunderous crash. *SMACK. The drywall spiders out in cracks.*

For a moment, the room keeps still, his hand frozen mid-air as his eyes widen in horror.

Nicholas reacts with pure-instinct, too. He collides into Chase within the second, before teleporting to a few feet above him. Falling, he drop-kicks Chase with a vicious blow. His brother tumbles to the carpet.

Landing on the boy's shoulders, he wraps his arms around the neck. *Constrict his breathing. Ease him into a peaceful stupor — a* fist to his head knocks Nicholas off, and the boy smacks to the floor. Chase scrambles to his feet. Ready to fight again. Nicholas rises to meet him, he's taken harder hits before.

Karmin is yelling, grabbing Chase's arm and pulling him back. Ellis runs to Ophelia, with Casey springing onto Nicholas.

"I know you can easily get out of this hold, but don't," he mumbles to his brother as their sister tries to calm Chase down. "Be the bigger person here, Nicholas."

Panting as Casey holds him back, he considers fleeing from his grasp and causing more damage. But Casey does have a point. He looks at him from the corner of his eye with a glare, before meeting Ophelia's gaze, then disappearing, surprising his siblings entirely.

Ophelia stands up slowly, her hand moving to the back of her head where blood flows. She grimaces, wiping her sticky fingers on her pant leg. "Chase, if I didn't care about your family so much, I would've put you in your place a long time ago." She stretches her shoulder, popping it back into place. "If I were truly the bad guy you assume I am, I wouldn't wait this long. I would've taken you out the second you opened your mouth."

***All the people you care about will soon learn, Zeitbombe*.**

That thought arrives from nowhere. How hard did she hit her head? Weird. "I'm going to go home now," she mumbles softly, "Gotta make sure I don't have a concussion."

Chapter 6

April 2023

She moves through the kitchen with an easy fluidity, a dancer's grace that defies the ground beneath her. Steam curls around her as she lifts the pot of boiling water from the stove, she pivots and carries it to the sink. She drains the pasta in one smooth motion, not a single splash touching her.

Before the steam even clears, she's already turning back to the stove. Her wooden spoon dips into the simmering sauce, stirring just enough to keep it from bubbling over. Then she's reaching for the pan on the back burner, adjusting the flame without looking, her body knowing the kitchen better than her eyes ever could.

Every movement is efficient. Controlled. A choreography of practiced gestures: open the cabinet, snag the colander, flip the pasta in the pot so it doesn't stick, check the garlic bread without pausing the sauce. She slides around the kitchen with a confidence that makes the chaos of boiling water, hot pans, and rising steam look almost elegant.

If existing was an art, Karmin Peters performs it like a dance.

Karmin pauses for just a moment, feeling eyes on her. Her younger brother, Ellis, sits wide-eyed at the kitchen island.

"You are the coolest person ever, and I've talked with the ghost of a pirate!" He exclaims excitedly.

Karmin raises a perfectly sculpted eyebrow. She's used to her brother's anecdotes about ghost conversations, but being called cool for making pasta was new. "It's just pasta, Eli."

"Yeah, but you were all..." He twirls his arms around. "Floaty!"

She laughs softly and starts to clean the counter, picking up discarded paper towels, tossing silverware into the sink. She's just about to throw away an untouched plate of cut-up hot dogs with mustard when Ellis stops her.

"No!"

Karmin's heterochromatic eyes—one brown, one bright orange—widen fractionally at her brother's shriek. She turns, coming face-to-face with his milky white, almost luminescent eyes.

She always thought his eyes looked like moonlight trapped behind glass.

Ellis puts his hands over the plate. "This isn't trash. It's for Jeremy and Alexius!"

"I thought ghosts can't eat?"

"They can't, but they like the smell. That's why they're usually always in the kitchen." He glances at the empty chairs beside him. "Father said I wasn't allowed to make food for them, but he never said anything about making food for myself and letting the ghosts smell it."

A sheepish smile spread across his face. "I think Mom thinks I'm going through a growth spurt with how much food she's seen me make."

Karmin's eyes shift between the plate of hot dogs and her brother. "So... do they like the smell of the spaghetti I'm making?"

Ellis cocks his head to the side and grins slowly. "Alexius says, 'It's sorcery the way she stirs the pasta with the confidence of a seasoned oracle.'" He pauses. "Jeremy says he usually burns pasta, so it smells great!"

Karmin laughs quietly, shaking her head as she moves back to the stove. "Well, you guys are always welcome to hang in the kitchen while I cook."

Chapter 7

Ophelia lays resting in her bed, mind in a whirlpool since her fight with Chase. So much chaos, and all caused by her. No matter how long she's known them, Chase refuses to warm up to her. She doesn't wish to give up, but at this point, if it doesn't happen now, it might never.

She doesn't want to cut contact with her friends just because of Chase. Ellis wouldn't want her to, and Karmin would be on her side, but Nicholas? She wasn't sure.

They are close and hang out daily, but Nicholas always thinks logically, tactically, never doing anything for his own emotional health. Maybe he only likes her around because she can be useful to his team?

Her anxiety starts to get the better of her, having her questioning everything she knows.

Her thoughts drown out any surroundings, though the house isn't holding that much stimuli to begin with. Swirling panic dulls the silence, the present fading around her. She relives past memories, trying to pinpoint any time she almost cost Nicholas his life. Was she on the path to losing her friends? Her best friend?

The walls of her bedroom become a temporary home for ice. She can't think clearly. What if—

Jolted by a small thud, her eyes flash open, the warmth returning to the room. Her eyes land on a nicely dressed boy at the edge of her bed.

"Nicky—" She breathes out. He cleaned up well after the fight, all the while she chose comfort in an oversized brown hoodie. She hopes he'll take over the conversation, her brain still racing, but she tries to focus on how her fingers feel against the soft blanket, and the comforting signature scent of the boy in front of her.

As the ice fades completely, Nicholas sighs. “We need to talk.” His jaw clenches, his gaze drifting down to the ground to his shoes speckled with dull crimson spots. The one item he failed to clean prior to his arrival. *Sloppy.*

He glances back up at her, attention solidifying entirely on her. “Are you okay?” Behind the weak tone, his question is... quiet. This weakness that rots the foundation of his pride lurks behind his breath.

The difference in his voice startles Ophelia. He always speaks so assertively, like he knows what he's doing and will kick your ass if you think otherwise. She mulls over the speech, momentarily forgetting the words. Has he taken down a wall with her?

"No one believes Chase." He assures, turning his back to her now as he paces the room, "I don't know why he decided to pick such a pointless fight. We all know you're not against us. But, I want to apologize on his behalf." A visibly shaky hand runs through his hair.

His lip catches between his teeth, his hands retreating back into their pockets. "I know we could've talked about this back at the house, but I thought it would mean more if I came to you alone... and with less blood on my person."

"Nicholas," She whispers softly, hoping to catch his attention and stop his nervous pacing. "I'm okay, a little sore, but I'll be fine."

Distracted by the photos on her wall, Ophelia relaxes at his lack of eye contact. "I'm glad no one agrees with Chase. I love being around you guys. I—uhm—" She pauses, crinkling her nose before deciding differently. "—I appreciate you coming here, and for cleaning up. You know that I can't focus when you're all bloodied. I can't help but try and tend to you myself."

She laughs at her words. "I mean, you're always thinking of me. Helping me when the noises get too loud, doing the more... *dirty* parts of our job so that I don't have to *hear* anything." She makes a face, shaking her head. "It's sweet. From the first moment I met you, you've always been there for me. That isn't something I'm willing to give up."

The subtle chime of Ophelia's voice emerges light from the darkness, suffocating the mist that embodies Nicholas's psyche. Sinking quickly until she rescues him. A temporary fix, and she brings him up to the surface to catch some air.

"For the record, I'm glad Chase didn't scare you off. I would've missed you. Really." His voice drips with sincerity. "You know... you're always there for me too." He presses his lips together in a thin line. "Maybe more than I'm there for you."

Who was she kidding, he always protects her on missions, always stays with her when her world crashes down. He listens to her rant and cry. She tries to return the favor, being there to pull him back from his work and getting him into the sun. "Yeah, we've always had each other's backs, huh?"

Nicholas sits down on the edge of the bed, leaning back on his hands for support. Was this what real friendship looks like? "Us against the world," he mutters, a lack of enthusiasm in his otherwise deadpan tone— Itching to say what he came here for. His stubbornness won't give in.

Ophelia pushes back the covers, sitting next to him with her legs crisscrossed. Her eyes trail over the side of his face, admiring how even his side profile looks perfect.

"I think Chase might have had a point. About you being a weakness for me—" He holds up a finger to keep her from potentially interrupting him. "— Not that that's necessarily a bad thing... but, it has been brought to my attention. I never noticed it before, until *he* pointed it out. I could care less what the old man says, but Chase… he's not smart enough to play mind games like that. What he said is true." He tilts his head, pressing his tongue to his cheek with his arms folding across his chest. "Either way, it doesn't matter, because I've noticed it too… I was just… denying myself." His voice sinks.

"I don't understand why I'm so stubborn. The only explanation I can conjure is that I simply am not used to feeling so… strongly about another person." The words spill out faster than he can slow them. He should stop, prevent himself from going any further, from a confession that she can brush off, kick him out for—

"I guess that's something we're good at, denying things and then getting worked up when someone points it out." Her voice hushes with a whisper. “Being stubborn is a way to protect yourself. Keeping out the change when you don’t know if it will be good or bad.”

Ophelia knows this can’t be what he wants, at least not right now. They have more pressing things to worry about. She lets him speak, gives him time to process in real time, before laying on her back with her gaze to the ceiling.

“If you didn’t have to be *this*, what would you do?” She starts softly, not *needing* to explain. “I like the idea that there are multiple realities out there. So, out there is a reality where we aren’t...”

Dangerous. She hates how people see her. How not only Chase, but how her father truly sees her as well. He built that ice chamber, he constantly sends her to her room during even the smallest disagreements between her and her siblings. She knows what he really thinks of her. She was tired of being seen that way.

"Emotions have consequences." He would say. She doesn't get it.

"I think I'd be a teacher," she continues, "Maybe work in a bookstore." The bed dips as he lays down next to her. "I'm not sure, but I know for certain that you're there. Us against the world, in every reality."

Nicholas smiles faintly, their eyes meeting. "You would make an excellent teacher."

He usually never gives into such aimless thoughts of hope, dreams leading him nowhere — he needs to focus on the *now*. But with Ophelia, he can't help but wonder.

"I think I would make a good barista... But I wouldn't trade that for what I have now," he clarifies,

"Even if we were to find each other, I like what we have now."

"Us against the world," she answers.

He smiles again. "Us against the world"

Chapter 8

July 2023

Last night had been another sleepless night. Another round of intense nightmares and premonitions that didn't make sense.

A girl with white in her hair screaming at him to help her.

A destroyed city with its buildings crumbled, citizens running in sporadic paths desperately trying to escape something.

Nicholas. Always Nicholas. The betrayal in his eyes. The twitch in his jaw.

Casey tiredly pushes open the door to his bedroom, only to stop short when he sees Nicholas inside, frozen like a deer caught in headlights.

“What are you doing in here, Nicholas?” Casey’s voice is quiet, the lack of sleep weighing heavy on him. His eyes dart around to make sure he’s in the right room.

He is.

Nicholas shrugs and shoves his hands in his pockets. “Your room needed a change.”

Casey’s heavy, deep brown eyes sweep around the room again. His bed is still unmade from his fitful night’s sleep. His walls are still blank, devoid of posters or decorations. He never knows what to put on them; he isn’t even sure if he has a favorite color or a hobby he likes. He likes sleep, though that rarely comes.

“What are you talking about, Nicholas?”

Wordlessly, Nicholas steps behind him and flicks the light switch.

The lights click off, and the room is swallowed by familiar darkness. For a moment, everything disappears into shadow. Then a soft green glow emerges, faint but steady, spilling from the small luminescent objects scattered across the ceiling. The walls, the furniture, even the edges of the carpet take on a muted emerald hue.

Above, the glow-in-the-dark stars dot the ceiling like frozen constellations. The steady green glow from the scattered stars gives the room a quiet, magical feeling, like stepping into a secret world, where everything feels safe.

"Glow-in-the-dark stars. I found them at a store," Nicholas mumbles, staring at the ceiling and avoiding his brother's gaze. "I got enough to cover the ceiling, and I organized those ones to look like the constellation Scutum." He gestures to a cluster

shaped like a narrow diamond. "Scutum looks like a shield... you know, for protection."

Casey's eyes stay locked on the constellation, tracing the pattern of the shield. "You... bought these for me?"

Nicholas snorts. "Sure, bought them." He shifts his weight, glancing at him. "If you don't like them—"

"No, this is really thoughtful. I didn't even know these things existed." Casey's voice is soft, his eyes never leaving the stars.

Nicholas gives a curt nod and steps toward the door. "I'll make sure no one bothers you for a few hours." With that, he slips out, closing the door quietly behind him.

Casey lies down on his bed, admiring the star-filled ceiling.

"Scutum... a shield," he whispers. "I didn't know constellations had meanings..."

Chapter 9

Chase paces the cold, hardwood floor, anger festering since the earlier incident. He doesn't understand why his siblings can still trust Ophelia after that failure of a mission.

He needs to do something to make Preston proud, he needs to prove that he's right, once and for all. Karmin hasn't talked to him lately, probably because Ophelia got to her too. How can she get everyone on her side, does she also have mind control powers, or something?

The home library can help him, it has anything and everything written about Thomas and his kids, right? Glancing around its giant shelves, he realizes he has no clue where to start. The 'everything' he seeks is made up of mostly news articles — No, he'll have to steal Preston's notebook to get what he needs. Well, not *he*. He doesn't dare go through his father's things. He wasn't Ellis.

Ellis.

Quickly, he runs back up to their bedrooms, bursting into that of his brother's.

"Ellis, buddy!" He calls out with a small smile, "Listen, I want to... apologize to Ophelia, and show her that I have truly changed. I want to get to know more about her, to surprise her—" he waits a moment to make sure the other is following. "—You know how Dad keeps that big book about us and his opponents in his office? Do you think you could go get that for me?"

Unsure what he needs to look for, he trusts that if this girl poses danger, Preston will know and would've written about it. Besides, it can't hurt to learn her weakness. "I'll give you $20?"

Ellis lays upside down on the edge of his bed, smirking. “Sure, Chase, I’ll do it.”

“Really?”

“Yeah, no problem.” He slides off the bed, laying on his back on the ground. “You’ll just have to repeat everything you just said. I only started paying attention when you mentioned money.”

Chase rolls his eyes. Typical.

Five minutes later, Ellis returns with a brown leather journal and a large grin. “I will take my money first.”

Chase sits uncomfortably in the desk’s chair, rolling his eyes and tossing him a 20. “Yeah, Yeah. Give me the book.” He snatches it and sets it upon the desk. The first page holds his father’s neat handwriting.

The OutKasts:

Subject: Rampage (Chase Peters): 17, Super Strength (Low threat.)

Subject: Nightmare (Casey Peters): 17, Dream-Memory Weaver: ability to project dreams, precognitive dreams (Low threat.)

Subject: Rogue (Nicholas Peters): 17, Teleportation (Medium threat but his combat skills pose a much larger threat.)

Subject: Nexus (Karmin Peters): 16, Emotion Sculpting: ability to solidify emotions into physical forms (Medium threat. Is getting better at making her anger into a blade but is still a reckless teen.)

Subject: Phantom (Ellis Peters): 16, Veil-piercing: ability to see both life and death (Low threat. Does not ever want to use his powers. A Waste.)

Chase's face falls at his father's description of him. He will show him he can be better than all his siblings, once he proves who Ophelia truly is. He flips through the pages, forcing himself to skip past Preston's takes on their training and missions. Finally, he lands on a page written in bold caps.

The OutKasts (O'Connor)

****Ages undetermined, as I am not their keeper.**

Tyler O'Connor: Super speed (Low threat.)

Elora and Alina O'Connor: Telekinesis (Must be near each other for power to work. Low threat.)

Parker O'Connor: Shape Shift (Medium Threat.)

Alice O'Connor: Mind Reader (Medium Threat.)

Ollie O'Connor: Flying (Low Threat.)

Megan O'Connor: Animal Transmutation (High Threat.)

Iris O'Connor: Plant Growth and Manipulation (Medium Threat.)

Cleo O'Connor: Pyrokinesis (High Threat. Seems unstable.)

Ophelia O'Connor: Chaos Magic and Cytokinesis (High Threat.)

-I fear that Ophelia O'Connor is the only O'Connor that possesses two powers, from my research, I gather that she gained both powers from her parents. Her chaos magic contains, but is not limited to: Reality Manipulation, Probability, Telekinesis, Energy Projection, Force Field Creation, and Spellcasting. I have conducted that she is unaware of the gravity of her powers due to the passing of her parents.

Chase studies the information, as if its uselessness will vanish. He already knows all this from seeing her perform during missions.

"This was pointless," he grumbles, slamming it shut. "There is nothing in this book that helps me."

"Yeah, that book looks boring compared to this one," Ellis says from the corner of his room, tracing a design on the thick red book he takes from behind his back.

"What? Let me see that."

Ellis holds the book up, the leather worn with jagged edges. At its center, an emblem of a storm cloud with fierce flames at its core glows with a rich gold. Embossed in bold, angular letters, ***Red Storm*** blares sharp and powerful, like lightning strikes. The fiery orange and red undertone letters flicker, as if burning.

This has to be what he needs. “Ellis, why didn’t you show me this earlier?” He takes a step forward, only stopping when his brother pulls the book back into his lap.

“Because, this book is clearly worth more than $20.” Ellis scoffs with a smirk. “I didn’t think you wanted it that badly. You wanted dad’s measly notebook.”

Chase groans. “Fine, I’ll give you another 20.”

Ellis shrugs softly, looking back at the cover. “This is such a pretty looking book. I might keep it.”

“You don’t read.” Chase spits out.

“Awe.” He clicks his tongue. “With that attitude, you won’t read this either.”

Chase glares at his brother, trying to keep it together. “Fine. Ellis,” he says slowly, “I’ll give you another 20, and I’ll do your chores for two weeks.”

"And you have to be nice to Ophelia."

Chase raises his eyebrow, grinning. "Sure, brother. Give me the book and I'll be nice to Ophelia too." He reaches into his pocket and hands him another 20.

Ellis beams, standing up to rip the bill from his hand. "Pleasure doing business with you. Now get out of my room." He pushes the book into Chase's chest before ushering him out.

Chase makes his way back to his room, shutting the door and taking his place at his desk. Once again, he begins to read.

Chapter 10

History of The Red Storm

Red Storm was a group of people who possessed chaos magic and elemental powers. Some elementals consisted of the basics: fire, water, and air, while others possessed lightning, light, or darkness. There is no known record of how or when the society came to be. Some believe that Red Storm were just a group of people who existed peacefully among regular people, while others believed they are the reason for all storms and other unexplainable phenomena. They believed they had the potential to bring on the end of the world.

The Red Storm united together under the shared interest of keeping their future generations safe among regular people. Despite never giving reason to believe that they were a superhero or villainous group, some people believed they held a secret alliance with the intention to rise up and take control.

The members created their name using the combination of both the chaos magic and elements that the group possessed. Red=Chaos, Storm= Elements. Their emblem became a way to recognize their own out in public. The group lived amongst regular humans in peace for years, until 1930 when Arthur Peters, an industrialist specializing in automobile and steel, fatally shot a man on his property. Peters claimed that the man was an elemental who came to his property, angry that he had been laid off, and tried to attack him. He shot in self-defense. Members of Red Storm stated that this man had not been an employee of Peters Industries, but simply a potential customer. With further investigation it became clear that the man had a Red Storm emblem embroidered on his pant cuff.

This sent a divide among the Red Storm members and some non-powered humans. Members were attacked in public, and even in their own homes, places of work, and schools. The Red Storm never initiated a fight, but were often jailed when standing up for themselves. Arthur Peters told people that The Red Storm would bring about the end of the world. He reported overhearing one of the members talking of one who would be called "Storm Soul" — a child brought into this world possessing both the powers of chaos magic and of the elements. Peters preached that they must eradicate Red Storm to keep Storm Soul from existing to protect the world.

After the massacre of a majority of the members, Red Storm went into hiding, no longer freely using their magic or displaying their emblem. Some believe that the members simply died out, others believe that they are still living amongst us, or even that they never existed in the first place.

Chase stops reading, staring at the page in front of him. There used to be super-humans just like him and his siblings. It was Preston's family that caused their downfall. He used to long for more people like him to connect with, but how can he now? The Red Storm must have had ulterior motives, why else would Arthur Peters attack that guy? Right?

Of course. His father, Preston Peters was a good and noble man, and so was Arthur.

He continues to skim the pages, gaze catching on his father's handwriting in the margins.

I have continued my search for the one they call Storm Soul and any other remaining Red Storm members. I have adopted five extraordinary children in hopes that one of them would be Storm Soul. I have come up empty. My nemesis, Thomas O'Connor, has adopted ten children. I have reason to believe that one of them is Storm Soul. I will do as my ancestors did, and do everything in my power to keep the world safe from the Red Storm.

Chase reread that part over again. Preston thought that Thomas had adopted whoever this Storm Soul was.

This Storm Soul would have both chaos and element magic. He goes over Thomas' kids in his head. Super speed, shape shifter, mind-reader— One of the daughters could control plants, does that count as an element?

Shoot. He'd left the other book in Ellis' room. *Come on now,* think. Super speed, shape shifter, mind-reader, plants, telekinesis... Ophelia. Ophelia has magic, he can't understand it, but her powers aren't confined to one. She can teleport, create portals and illusions. That's magic.

He thought back to a mission long ago where Ophelia had used her magic to summon a dagger, but instead of using magic, she created this weapon. With ice. Ice was an elemental, wasn't it? Ophelia O'Connor was the Storm Soul. Ophelia was going to bring about the end of the world. His father knew this, or at least had his suspicions. Now Chase knew, and he would make sure everyone realized the game she was playing.

Especially Nicholas.

Before he closed the book, he noticed a yellow sticky note stuck to one of the pages, with his father's handwriting scribbled across.

Dangerous. If Storm Soul experiences too strong of any negative emotion they could alter the weather. Too much could be deadly.

Time Bomb.

“Forty bucks and no chores for a week.” Ellis mused happily after shutting the door on Chase. He shoves the money in his pocket and walks further into his room when he notices the notebook still on his desk.

He rolls his eyes annoyed that his brother had forgotten it. “Okay father Preston. What secrets are you writing about your lovely children.” He snatches the book off the desk, flopping down on the bed on his back. He flips through the pages musing over some of the notes.

“Ha! Low threat Chase!” He laughs to himself. “I’m better at Chase than something. Wonder if I can get this framed.”

He continues to flip through the book, getting rather bored of the contents until he saw Ophelia's name written in his father's handwriting. There were a few passages, most were in Preston's signature neat and precise handwriting, but more recent passages looked rushed. Ellis tilts his head to the side and sits up.

- I have had my suspicions for a while that Helena Aldane would give birth to the Storm Soul. I have watched her work as a librarian downtown. I tried countless times to get her husband, Archer Aldane to work at my company, but he denied saying he was happy with his role as a Cryogenic Technician.

-I have continued to keep an eye on the couple and found that Helena has in fact given birth to a baby girl. They call her Ophelia. As of now there is no sign of this child possessing both magic and elemental powers.

- I have adopted five children. There are six children in my home now. One is peculiarly worrisome, is it possible I possessed the Storm Soul all along?

-This child, whom my wife insists I refer to as Abigail, has become a pain. She is not my Storm Soul, but possesses the power of manipulation, and she is very hard to control. I must figure out what to do with her.

- The other five will serve their purpose just fine.

- Helena and Archer are dead. I should have struck earlier, before the birth of their daughter. I left room for error and for that I brought shame to my family's name, but with the death of Helena and Archer I hope to restore my family pride even just a bit. I caught them in their home, I was moments from getting to their daughter, now 12, when Thomas walked in. (What he was doing here he would not share). We fought, and he won knocking me unconscious. When I awoke the girl was gone.

- Thomas has adopted the girl. I told him there was nothing stopping her from seeking revenge for the death of her parents, and it would be best for him to let me finish what I started. He said there was no need for that, as he erased her memories of that night, and of her parents entirely.

- I must find a way to deal with this Storm Soul without raising suspicions. No one has figured out the murder of the Aldane's and thus the case has been closed. This works in my favor, however, it makes it much harder for me to go about my original plan.

- I must be more shrewd. The kids go on missions, and missions are constantly failing.

"Holy..." Ellis mumbles quietly. Preston killed Ophelia's parents, and she has no memory of it because Thomas erased her memory. He had no clue what the Storm Soul meant, there was no mention of it elsewhere in the notebook. He didn't know why he killed her parents, or what purpose they were meant to serve. He also grew curious of this Abigail child, he only had one sister and that was Karmin.

Ellis stands up and paces his room. "I need to tell someone this," he mumbles. He didn't trust Chase, Nicholas was most likely still angry, Karmin would scold him for sneaking around in his father's office. That left Casey.

Quickly Ellis shoves the notebook under his shirt and awkwardly runs to Casey's room. He knocks quickly and spoke in a hush tone. "Casey!

Casey open up!" His eyes look down the hallway towards Chase's door hoping he wouldn't come out.

The door swings open and a groggy Casey glares out at Ellis. "What. Do you want." He says drowsily.

"I know I know we're not supposed to bother you between 2:30 and 5:00—" He starts.

"And it's 3:15 so you better have a great reason for waking me up." He snaps.

Guilt twists in his stomach, feeling bad for waking his brother. Casey needed more sleep due to his powers causing him mental fatigue. Ellis knows it's rare for his brother to not dream without catching a glimpse of the future. But the tone in his voice tells him that this was one of those times. And that means he needs to bring up the more troubling information he's found and talk about this Abigail person later.

"I know. I'm sorry. This is important, it's about dad." He lowers his voice, "And a secret he's kept."

Casey rolls his eyes. "That old man keeps tons of secrets, none of them are worth waking me up for." He starts to close the door before Ellis blurts out,

"It's about Ophelia!"

Casey pauses behind the partially closed door, sighing heavily before swinging it open allowing his brother in. "Make it quick."

Ellis steps inside, his eyes trying to adjust to the darkness that covers the room. That was cut short when Casey flicked on the switch, light chasing away the darkness.

"What about Ophelia?" He grumbles.

"Preston killed her parents!" Ellis whispers with wide eyes.

"What?" His mind scrambles for more to say. "How do you know that? How do you know anything about her parents? She doesn't even know about them, she says they gave her up when she was a baby." Just like him. It was one of the things he could relate to with her. While some of the others lost their parents or simply just didn't know their origin story, Casey knew that his parents were unfit to raise him, giving him up without a second thought.

"I read it in this," Ellis says as he pulls the notebook out from under his shirt.

"Why do you have dad's notebook?"

"Chase needed it."

He blinks. "Why did Chase need it?"

"I don't know," he mumbles quickly, waving his hand away. "Here look!" He thrusts the book into his brother's hands.

Casey's eyes scan over the passage quietly, his face never giving away his thoughts. He looks up at his brother. "Why on earth would he do that? And what the hell is Storm Soul?"

"I don't know!" He exclaims. "I don't know! The only thing in that book is notes about our powers and how we're doing during trainings and missions. That's the only page that talks about Ophelia or this "Storm Soul" thing."

Casey furrows his eyebrows and looks down at the page again. "What does this mean about missions going wrong?" He flips through the pages. "This isn't even the most recent passage either. This was written when Ophelia was 12," he says slowly. "Has Preston been trying to kill us on missions?"

Ellis shakes his head, "No, I don't think so. I mean, a lot of our missions have been fairly easy, and whatever looks good for the press. The most dangerous mission was..." He trails off meeting his brother's eyes.

"Today's mission." Casey finishes. "The one mission where dad wasn't specific on the task, the one mission where he specifically requested that Ophelia joins."

It doesn't make any sense to Casey. If Preston held this disdain for Ophelia since she was 12, why wait to harm her five years later?

"What are we supposed to do?" Ellis whispers.

"I don't know!"

"You haven't gotten any dreams or anything about dad or Ophelia? Anything?"

He shakes his head. "My dreams sometimes show far into the future and are very short. Very rarely are they about near-future events. They don't always make sense." He sighs, thinking for a moment. "My dream last night, I couldn't see anything. It was just foggy."

Ellis tilts his head. "Like the building earlier?"

Casey blinks, then drops his gaze down to the ground. "I wish I had known that earlier. I could've helped us." He slowly sinks to the edge of his bed.

"How were you supposed to know what was going to happen in a dream based off of fog? You couldn't have known." Ellis spoke softly, pausing for just a moment. "But I think I have an idea on how you can help us now."

Casey lifts his head to meet his eyes. "How?"

He points to the notebook. "Preston said that Thomas erased Ophelia's memory of her parents and what happened to them. That memory could still be present, all you have to do is—"

"No!" Casey snaps standing up. "Don't even finish. I'm not doing that!"

"Casey, you're the only one who can help someone regain memories," he says slowly.

"It doesn't matter. I won't do that again. I won't do it to her."

Ellis goes quiet for a moment. "Nicholas knows it wasn't your fault."

Casey closes his eyes, trying not to think of that night. Preston had been angry with the kids for not excelling during one of their training sessions. He was particularly hard on Nicholas, calling him sloppy. When Nicholas started to argue with Preston, their father told Casey to inflict punishment on his brother.

Casey tried hard to fight against it, but eventually he gave into his father's harsh demands. He made a memory that Nicholas had pushed down deep, rise to the surface. Casey felt Nicholas's feelings with an indescribable intensity, he saw what he was reliving.

What was worse was that Casey was never able to shake the memory of his brother's face.

Nicholas's face was cold, unreadable as usual. His eyes were distant, posture rigid, and breathing even. But then, the memory started to sink in. Casey could see his brother's jaw tighten, and his eyes flicker, and a fleeting expression of pain flashed across his face, gone almost as quickly as it appeared.

Casey noticed him slightly flinch, his brows furrowed. He witnessed his brother's cold, controlled mask slip. His lips twitched but he was trying to fight to keep it hidden. Nicholas's eyes narrowed, his gaze far away. Casey barely noticed the small, involuntary tremor in his hands, how his chest was rising and falling slightly faster, his breath shallow, as if he was struggling to hold it together.

The memory faded and finally the mask settled back into place, but there's something different now. His coldness was more pronounced. The vulnerability that briefly escaped had been locked away again, but the heaviness remained. Casey felt it.

Nicholas didn't talk to him for weeks, and even now it seemed that the brothers' relationship was never the same.

Ellis could see that right now Casey was reliving that moment. "You would've been punished if you didn't." He reminds him. "Nicholas knew that. We all did."

"It wasn't right of me," he whispers. "I should've taken it."

Ellis shakes his head. "It wasn't right of Preston to do that. He shouldn't put us against each other like that."

Casey hands back the notebook. "Nicholas's memory wasn't a forgotten memory, and that alone was emotional for him. I can't imagine what it would do to Ophelia. She has no memory of this, and if she learns about her parents, what would that do for her? She can't fix it." He pauses, "We don't even know if I *can* bring back that memory."

Ellis looks at the book before taking it. "I know you can, Casey, your powers are strong, and you care about Ophelia. That has to count for something." He caught his brother's eyes. "If someone had information about your parents and why you weren't with them, wouldn't you want to know?"

Casey's eyes flicker to the notebook, then up at Ellis, then back at the notebook. "Please leave Ellis, I need to take a nap," he mumbles walking to the door. "Put the notebook back before you get caught."

Chapter 11

The doughnut shop sat on the corner like a sun-bleached postcard from another decade—cheerful and stubbornly proud of its own charm. The exterior was a low, boxy building painted a soft pastel pink. A striped mint green and cream awning drooped lazily over the entrance.

*Above it all towered the sign: a giant doughnut perched on a pole, glossy and golden as if lacquered in sugar. Beneath the pastry, two rectangular signs jutted out at slightly mismatched angles, their retro lettering reading **"Darla's"** and **"Devine Donuts!"** The bulbs around the edges had long since given up on glowing.*

Inside, the shop was a time capsule. Checkerboard tiles—white and cherry red—

stretched across the floor, scuffed from years of customers shuffling in for morning coffee or after-school treats.

The counter gleamed, its stainless-steel surface reflecting rows of doughnuts behind glass: powdered, glazed, chocolate dipped, jelly filled. A faded menu board with magnetic letters announced the day's specials.

Booths upholstered in turquoise vinyl hugged the walls, their cushions cracked from thousands of conversations. The jukebox in the corner hadn't been touched since the diner closed at 7 p.m.

"My favorite sugary universe, where every bite tastes like someone saved a piece of the past just for you!" Ellis says, spinning with his arms in the air.

Casey snorts. "You should pitch that to Darla for her marketing campaign."

Karmin hums. "I like it. Very... poetic."

Chase crosses his arms, leaning against the back door he came through. "I don't know why you lot teleport when Darla literally gave us a key." He holds it up before tucking it into his pocket.

Nicholas strides past him, heading straight for the display of doughnuts Darla left for them. "It's more fun to feel like you're breaking and entering."

"I think we should just be happy Darla lets us come here after hours," Casey says, glancing around like he expects their father to materialize. "She trusts a group of teenagers not to destroy her business."

"We're not just a group of teenagers, now are we, Casey?" Karmin lifts the glass lid and retrieves a jelly filled doughnut.

"Yeah, we're far from normal!" Ellis exclaims, grabbing a maple bear claw.

Chase sighs and joins them, looking over the pastries. "I think what Karmin means is we're basically this city's equivalent of superheroes. We have no reason to destroy a mom-and-pop doughnut shop."

"Yeah! We save that for the big corporations!" Ellis says through a mouthful.

Nicholas silently hands Ophelia a strawberry doughnut before leaning against the wall and taking a bite of his own.

Ellis steals a bite of hers. "Strawberry maple!"

Ophelia snatches it back. "Sir, that is illegal."

"Not really! Our love is too strong!" He swallows dramatically. "A moment without you is like an eternity passed."

"Why do you always get poetic when you're doing something you shouldn't be?"

"Because someone has to be the profound one in this family!"

Karmin laughs behind her hand. "Profound? Ellis, earlier today you told Preston that if he drove 106 instead of 45, we'd get home faster."

"I stand by that," Ellis says lazily.

Nicholas wipes his hands. "Alright, oh wise one, what were your thoughts on today's mission?"

Ellis licks frosting off his fingers, thinking. "I thought the guy with the red hair was nice."

"The hostage?" Nicholas blinks. "You saw him for like ten seconds."

"He was nice for those ten seconds."

"You're impossible." Chase rubs his forehead.

"Impossible, but I'm the one who charmed Darla into giving us afterhours access," Ellis says with a wink. "You're welcome."

Chase rolls his eyes but can't hide a small smirk. "She probably felt bad because you tripped over air the day she met you."

Ellis blushes. "I—I was tripped! By a ghost!"

They burst into laughter.

Karmin giggles. "Remember how you used to blame ghosts for everything?"

Casey joins in. "'Ellis, who started this small fire?' 'It was the 18th-century poet! He wanted inspiration!'"

Chase snorts. "'Ellis, why are you hiding in the dumpster?' 'The Viking told me to!'"

Ellis smiles sheepishly but proud. "To be fair, Ivar did bet me I couldn't last five minutes. We had a lively conversation about Viking grooming. He was not a fan of the wolf-urine myth."

Ophelia brightens. "Are there any ghosts in here right now?"

Ellis rubs the back of his neck. "Well... there's a lady singing opera in the corner. And an older man reading a paper from the '20s." His eyes drift to a darkened corner.

Nicholas stiffens immediately. "Is something bad over there?"

Ellis shakes his head. "No, it's some old man grumbling about darn kids eating his doughnuts. Also, he hates Chase's haircut."

Chase straightens and gestures toward the door. "I've had enough for tonight."

Karmin follows and calls back, "See even the ghost hate Chase's hair!"

"Karmin, don't," Nicholas mutters as he herds everyone out into the night.

Chapter 12

Karmin Peters runs silently down the long hallway, her feet quietly padding along the hardwood floor. She has waited for this moment for months.

She slides to a stop at Ellis's door, opens it, and slips inside, quickly shutting the door behind her, Ophelia and her three brothers greeting her. "Are you guys ready?" A wide grin plasters itself on her warm brown skin.

"Yes!" Ellis says excitedly.

"Are you sure he's gone?" Casey spoke worriedly.

Nicholas stays leaning against the wall, his eyes trained on the door behind his sister.

"Yes, he's gone out of town for the night. Mom is in bed." Karmin's grin never leaves her face. "Let's go." She walks to Ellis's window above his bed, shimming it open.

"Why do we always have to sneak out the window? Two of us can just teleport," Nicholas says, watching her.

"It's part of the experience," Karmin replies, climbing down the ladder.

"Yeah Nicky, it's a part of the fun." Ophelia smirks, walking over to the window.

Nicholas rolls his eyes, pushing himself off the wall, snatching the bag of towels, careful not to leave it behind, before following her out the window.

The tall mansion stands looming over the city block. The gleaming marble and intricate stonework seemed to demand attention, with its massive windows that catch the sunlight and shimmer like a beacon. Its towering structure casts long shadows over the nearby shops and apartments.

Nicholas always thought this was an unapologetic testament to Preston's ego's need for attention.

Ellis was the last one to come down after Casey. "Why is Chase not coming again?"

The night air is cool and smells of damp earth and adventure. The world outside seems so much bigger in the still of the night.

"Because we don't like him." Nicholas huffs, ignoring the glare from his sister.

"You know Chase was never a fan of all this. We're just lucky he doesn't tell Preston." She reminds him.

"Daddy's boy." Nicholas mutters.

The group makes their way towards a dark and narrow alley, the only light being the faint glow of a nearby streetlamp and the moonlight. One at a time, they pull their bikes from behind a stack of old wooden crates and rusted trash cans, the metal frames creaking slightly after a while of being hidden away.

They mount their bikes, the quiet alley now fills with the sound of wheels spinning, pedals clicking, and their nervous, excited laughter. After a quick nod from Nicholas, they shot out of the alley like a group of fireflies escaping the dark, their tires hitting the pavement with a soft thud as they race into the night.

The quiet streets now fill with the laughter and hollering of the teens as they speed down the road. Nicholas and Ophelia were weaving their bikes past each other in a crisscross motion, Casey and Karmin were racing, and Ellis was trying to pop a wheelie.

"Race you guys to the bridge!" Casey yells to the group before speeding ahead.

"You're on!" Ellis yells peddling past Karmin to catch up to his brother.

They speed down the quiet street, the soft buzz of the streetlights guiding their way. No plans, no obligations, just the thrill of feeling free. A single moment where life wasn't demanding more than they could give.

The wind stings their faces as they zoom through the familiar streets, remembering how they had snuck out to race down these same streets anytime that their father was out of town for business. Tonight was for forgetting about everything else and just being themselves. No rules. No codenames. Just them being teenagers.

Casey arrives to the old bridge near the edge of town first, Ellis then Karmin following, lastly Ophelia and Nicholas who weren't actually racing.

Casey let his bike crash down to the ground as he runs towards a few tall, tangled bushes. "Did you remember, Ophelia?" He sticks his arm into the bush, feeling around.

"Of course, I did," she says setting her bike down on the ground carefully.

Finally, Casey was able to grab ahold of what he was looking for. He pulls out a large picnic basket, that Ophelia had hidden in the bushes earlier, filled with all kinds of sweets and sugary drinks.

"There better be chocolate cookies in here" Ellis mutters kneeling down next to his brother, rifling through the basket with him. "Yes!" He says pulling out a container of chocolate cookies.

"You have to share that, Ellis!" Casey argues reaching for it.

The boys wrestle for the cookie container, Karmin steps over them and pulls out another container of Carmel brownies and a bottle of red fizzy soda. "Tell your mom I said thanks for this, Ophelia," she says sitting down at the edge of the bridge.

Ophelia and her mother always made sweets for the kids when they knew Preston would be out of town. He rarely used their actual names; sweets were out of the question.

Ellis and Casey now sit against the tree eating out of the container together.

"Remember when I dared Casey to jump into the creek?" Ellis laughs brushing cookie crumbs from his mouth. "He was so scared!"

"I was not!" Casey defended. "I was being cautious, it was dark."

Ellis laughs harder holding up his hands as his brother shoves his shoulder.

"I remember when Nicholas had us race up the rocky path... and—" Karmin says now in between laughter. "—We were so confused on how he started out behind all of us but always managed to win. He was teleporting the whole time!"

Nicholas leans against the tree that Ophelia sits under, smirking proudly as Karmin finishes her story. "It's called adapting."

"It's cheating." Casey chuckles shaking his head.

Ophelia smiles against the mouth of her blue fizzy soda bottle, taking a quick swig before holding it up for Nicholas to take. "His punishment was jumping in the freezing cold water." She laughs as well remembering the annoyed face of a soaking wet Nicholas.

Nicholas rolls his eyes and picks up the bottle, he inspects the liquid, swirling it around before taking a small sip. He crinkles his nose, making a face before handing it back. "It wasn't a punishment, it was an ambush." He points out, "Casey came out of nowhere and shoved me."

Casey nods with a small smirk. "Anytime."

The kids finished with their snacks and their story times and were now gathered on the bridge. All except Nicholas and Ophelia who keep to the tree.

"I bet I could guess your favorite color." She tells him, her eyes staying on the three siblings who had made their way to the bridge.

Nicholas didn't have a favorite color. "Go ahead."

Ophelia turns her head to look up at him "Dark Red," she says confidently. "Or at least it's the color that looks best on you." She gestures to his dark red sweater.

Nicholas stays quiet just looking at the excitement etched on her face at her guess. He didn't get a chance to tell her she was wrong. Or that now she was right, or tell her anything because she ran off to the bridge to join the others.

The wooden planks creak beneath their feet, Ellis leans over the rusty railing, peering down at the dark water below, the gently rippling water mesmerizing him. He climbs onto the ledge as he stretches his arms wide. "Last one in is a coward!" he yells, his voice breaking the stillness of the night. Without hesitation, he leapt, his body arching in the air before splashing into the cool water below with a loud "whoop!"

Karmin leans over the edge and watches him land in the water. Her hands quickly pull her curly hair into a bun on the top of her head. "You're insane!" She shouts, laughing breathlessly, but the excitement in her voice betrays her. She climbs onto the edge, closes her eyes, and pushes off, a splash swallowing her echoing scream.

Ophelia couldn't help but laugh at the infectious sounds of her friends' laughter. She watches the two splash each other before looking at Casey. She nudges him and grins. "You said you would do it this time."

"I never said I'd *like* it," Casey mutters watching his siblings below.

"Come on Case, you can trust me." She promises giving him a soft smile. "You'll have fun, and we can jump together." She steps on the ledge and reaches for his hand. "We've both been through worse than what's down there," she says softly, her eyes searching his. "The world never gave us anything but reasons to be afraid. But right now, we jump with no fear. Together."

He takes a breath before stepping up to the ledge, his legs shaking slightly. He glances down at the water, then back at Ophelia. "Together." He nods before taking the plunge with her. He let out a shout that turns into laughter mid-air.

The coolness envelops Casey completely, shocking his senses awake. His initial panic melts away as his feet instinctively kick, propelling him upward. He breaks through the surface, gasping for air, only to hear Ophelia's laughter echoing nearby. The sound felt warm, alive, and infectious, cutting through the chill like a lifeline.

He turns to find her grinning at him, her curls plastering to her face and water dripping from her chin. "See?" Ophelia says, her voice breathless but steady. "Maybe this will be a nice memory for you to always remember when you need it."

Ophelia knows how hard it is on Casey to have those dreams, knows how it hurts him when

Preston makes him use his powers against his siblings. Ophelia hopes that if she could help him make more good memories, it would take the sting out of the bad ones.

Casey stares at her, speechless. He thought back to Ellis and his plan to help Ophelia remember. Here she was, this warm girl who had been protected from such a cruel memory, did he dare bring that back for her? Would he want to know about his own parents? It was rare to see Ophelia not her smiling, bubbly self, he couldn't be the one to take that from her.

"Jump!" Ophelia screams happily up at Nicholas who was peering over the bridge. "Are you a coward?!"

Nicholas rolls his eyes. "I'm not a coward, I'm just not stupid enough to get my clothes wet and have to trek water back to the house."

"Clothes dry, and memories are forever!" She says, the other kids swimming towards her chanting "Jump! Jump!"

Nicholas didn't move. "I don't give into peer pressure," he replies coolly. Though, he couldn't help but look at Ophelia's face flushed with excitement, her wide eyes gleaming. He wanted to be down there and experience what she was experiencing. He wasn't sure he could, she always seemed to have a different perspective than him when it came to just about anything. Nicholas glances up at the moon then down at his family in the water, then he walks off the bridge.

He walks back over to the tree, ignoring the *boos* from the kids down below, pulls off his sweater, folding it neatly on the ground, and then goes back to the bridge. He climbs to the ledge and jumps in.

The freefall feels endless, the weight of the world lifting off his shoulders for just a moment.

He hits the water and lets it envelop him, he doesn't fight it, instead he let the water pull him under. The world above growing quieter, dimmer, until there's nothing but the muffled hum of the creek around him.

Suspended in the dark, he let himself sink, arms floating weightlessly at his sides. Welcoming the cold pressing in, numbing the ache. A fleeting escape from the heaviness that's always there.

His eyes remain open, watching the distorted world above, the rippling moonlight fractured and unreachable. Thoughts flood in, clearer here in the silence than they've been in years. For a moment, he stays like that, suspended between the surface and the depths, caught between who he was and who he was trained to be. The water feels like a cocoon, a barrier that keeps the world at bay. But even here, in this fleeting sanctuary, he knows he can't stay.

He allows himself to be jealous, just for a moment, of his siblings and of Ophelia. They were all dealt the same cards, parents who had given them up for one reason or another, him and his siblings having more of a dictator than a father, never being able to experience being a normal teen. Yet somehow, they still managed to enjoy what they could, they didn't grow cold and calculating, they weren't paranoid. He could never get himself to act like that, warm, trusting, emotional. Even now as he floats weightlessly in the dark.

With a deep, deliberate breath, he kicks his legs and propels upward, breaking through the surface in a rush of air and cold. The world greets him again, loud, bright. Overwhelming. He watches Ellis and Karmin scramble back up to the bridge to jump again, he notices Casey cheering them on from the water below.

He continues to scan the rippling water until his eyes land on her. Floating on her back, Ophelia drifts weightlessly in the gentle current of the creek.

The icy water seems to kiss her deep brown skin, but she doesn't shiver. She lets it hold her, cradling her like an endless embrace. Her snowy white curls spread around her head like a glowing halo, damp but luminous under the soft silver light of the moon.

Her eyes stay on the sky that stretches endlessly, and its tapestry of stars. Her chest rising and falling slowly, matching the rhythm of the water's flow as she let her eyes trace the constellations, connecting the dots in her mind.

Her fingers skim the water lazily, sending ripples outward. She closes her eyes for a moment, letting the coolness of the water seep into her, grounding her. Here, under the vast sky, she felt safe. Here and now, she was not the most dangerous thing in the waters of this infinite ocean.

She then let her body sink slightly into the water, the coolness of the water ripples against her arms as she starts to tread lightly, her feet kicking slowly beneath the surface. She catches Nicholas's gaze and grins softly. "Did you see it?"

He glances away, slightly embarrassed that she caught him looking at her. "See what?" His eyes trail back over to hers.

"The shooting star," she whispers softly, a small smile on her face. "I've never seen one before, it's amazing."

He raises his eyebrow at that comment. He didn't care much about the science that was shooting stars, nor did he classify it was something amazing. "Why is that?"

Ophelia shrugs softly. "It's a piece of meteor that is burning up by the Earth's atmosphere. Seeing something falling from the sky, burning, would be seen as scary, it could be dangerous." She hums softly, "But people don't see it that way. Instead, it gets to burn not with the scorch of danger, but with the soft glow of being loved." She was a storm contained within a fragile frame, a power that threatened to break free with every breath. People only saw the energy, the danger, the risk. They saw the flash, the power, but never the person beneath it. She pulls her gaze away from the sky and back towards him "You didn't get to see it did you?"

"Yeah..." he says quietly "I did."

The kids walk the quiet streets, pulling their bikes alongside them. None of them spoke, but they don't need to, each knows they are dreading the same thing. Morning, when Preston is home and they were back to their world of training, codenames, fear.

"Do you ever think about what happens if we get caught?" Casey asks quietly, the house coming into view.

Karmin shrugs, glancing at the sky above. "We'll handle it together. But during these nights? We're kids again. We get to worry about normal kid things."

They hide their bikes before climbing back up the ladder into Ellis's window.

Nicholas had already stashed his bike and was walking Ophelia and her bike back to her own house.

Ellis shuts his window and turns around to see Casey right behind him. Karmin must have gone back to her room. "You okay Casey?"

"I don't want to let Ophelia down." He whispers quietly, not able to meet his brother's eyes.

"What do you mean?"

He frowns softly and looks at him. "I would want to know about my parents. I know she does too, she talks about who they could've been," his voice was still quiet, "I don't want her to never know, to live like that. I don't want Preston to use it to hurt her." He shakes his head. "I *can't* be the one to hurt her. I can't let him do that to her."

Ellis nods softly. "Okay. How do we do this?"

Casey takes a deep breath. "I'll pull the memory up as a dream. It will be less overwhelming to her if she's asleep, easier to process."

Ellis simply nods.

"But whatever happens, we can't let Preston tell her first."

Chapter 13

Nicholas sits on top of an old car, it's brown paint chipped and worn. This car sits in the middle of a beautiful, vibrant flower field, far from the normal scenic view of his bedroom where he had been just hours before Ophelia appeared in his room to drag him on a spontaneous picnic outing.

Earlier when he had asked where this destination was, he was a bit discouraged to learn that she had no idea of its exact location, admitting to him that she had found it accidentally during a power malfunction on a particularly stressful day. He only agreed because he would make sure to observe their surroundings. He does this upon arrival... such beauty needing to be taken in. It was strikingly different than what he had normally surrounded himself with.

His hands clasp the half empty container of pasta that Ophelia had packed. “You said you come here often?”

“Mhm,” Ophelia says in between bites of her own pasta. “The first time was a complete accident, but I started coming here more and more just to clear my head. Sometimes after training, sometimes when I can’t sleep, when my house feels overcrowded.” She lifts her head up, closing her eyes for a moment to feel the sun on her face. “It’s quiet and at night you can see so many stars.”

Even now during the daytime, this flower field provides a sense of calm to the girl, and she was thankful she could share it with the boy who also provides her with that same sense of calm. “I haven’t told anyone but you. I don’t want it to lose its magic.”

He finishes his pasta, snapping the lid back into place before stacking it neatly in its original spot in the basket. "Magic? Really?" He grins, "I think there can be beauty in nature without magic."

She rolls her eyes "Yes magic. Of course there *can* be beauty in nature without magic. Who's to say that all magic is beauty?" She questions. "The most beautiful thing could be deadly." Her eyes trail across his face, admiring his side profile before looking at her pasta container.

He glances at her and lets this perfect moment settle over him. However, everything that *seemed* perfect was usually anything but. His thoughts keep trailing back to Chase and how adamant he was that the girl that currently sits beside him was planning to betray them.

Ophelia breathes out "This is nice. Not having to worry about your siblings bothering us with their teasing or demands of help." She chuckles softly. "Or mine coming to interrogate you."

A breeze starts to pick up in the field, the scent of fresh flowers was enough to make him sneeze. For the sake of his own embarrassment, he does everything in his power to keep from doing so. He nods in agreement but couldn't quiet the thoughts that yell at him, telling him that she was learning his weaknesses, and would use them against him. He was trying hard to enjoy what time they had left.

"It is very nice," he whispers quietly. He now starts to make his way off the car. "I hope you don't mind my abrupt departure, we should come here again sometime."

Ophelia raises her eyebrow. "What?" Her feelings were a bit hurt as he was ready to leave so quickly. "Is something wrong?"

Nicholas did think that everything was going smoothly but this comfort wasn't something he allowed himself to indulge in. Not because he felt he is greater than a picnic in a flower field, but rather he simply felt he couldn't accept this serenity that takes over his life.

It was new. Alarming. This girl had rearranged his regular schedule, making more time to see her, allowing more smiles to come from him, she had changed him more than he'd like to admit. He hates admitting it again, but Chase was right. Ophelia made him weak.

His regular unsettling grin pulls at his lips. "I think my siblings are up to something stupid. I for one don't want to miss the front row seat." He disappears in that pale green light.

Nicholas sits at his desk, fully engrossed in a book before being interrupted by an aggressive knock on his door. He simply ignores it, eyes never leaving the pages, only to have Chase swing open the door with no remorse.

His eyes lift from the page, jaw tightening. He doesn't say anything at first, just watches his brother walk in uninvited. "You could knock," he says finally, the irritation sharp in his voice. Then, after a beat, "You have exactly three seconds to explain what the hell you want, Chase."

Chase pushes past him, slamming a dark red book down on the desk, the wood slightly cracking from the pressure. "Ophelia is dangerous!" he says flipping through the pages. "Ellis found this in father's study and look—" He shows him the sticky note that he found. "—Apparently if she feels too much of a negative emotion, she can alter the weather. It could get really bad really fast. He compared her to a time bomb."

Nicholas stares at his brother in disbelief at how unremorseful he seems about barging into his room. His eyes dart over to Ellis who was awkwardly standing in the doorway. He rolls his eyes, opting to hear him out only because he spoke about Ophelia.

"Oh what, you can *read* now? Is that your groundbreaking discovery? I don't need any more opinions from a neanderthal." He spits, quickly turning away from him and his book.

"I'm not the only one who thinks she's bad news, *Rogue*. Dad thinks so too, and he's not wrong.

There is information about Ophelia, and something called a *Storm Soul.*" He waves his hand around. "You've been spending so much time with her that she probably got in your head. She probably knows your weaknesses." He pauses, straightening his posture. "Probably knows ours too. You are just some kind of pawn in her game. What I can't figure out is if she is the master or just a piece to something bigger."

Nicholas clenches his jaw at Chase's use of the codename. He makes his way over to the book, stepping past Chase to quickly study the pages. He wouldn't admit it, but it made his stomach turn with anxiety. He slams the book closed. "This is ridiculous."

"Ridiculous!?" Chase sputters. "She is a weapon, and she will kill you. I'd also mention that she'll kill us, but I know you don't care about anyone but yourself." Chase can't understand why someone like Ophelia would willingly spend so much time with someone like Nicholas. He isn't capable of caring about anyone, so the only logical reason was that she has him under mind control.

Nicholas throws his hands up in mock surrender. "I can't do this right now—" He rubs his head and closes his eyes taking a deep breath. Clapping his hands together to create an arrow, which he points at Chase. "—Chase. Look at me, are you even hearing yourself?" His lips press into a tight grin. "What is the point of this? Is this your pitiful excuse to get everyone working against Ophelia so you can feel like you have control? Hate to break it to you, that's not going to happen."

Casey appears slowly in the doorway. His tired eyes staring at Nicholas. "Have you seen Ophelia today? I need her to know about this dream I had." He walks into the room to lean against the wall. "I hope she's okay."

Nicholas ignores his drowsy brother, eyes fixed ahead, jaw tight. Her name lingers, but he doesn't answer. First things first and that means dealing with the brother who just called her dangerous. "Chase. Enough is enough. I know that Preston seriously messed you up, but this is a new level, even for you. So, stop with the allegations and theories—" He closes his eyes and sighs a low groan. "—Just let me be happy for once."

Ophelia appears in the middle of the room, eyes wide and unfocused, hands twisting at the hem of her shirt.

"Ophelia!" Ellis says happily rushing over. "Casey had a dream about you— Wait, can everyone else see her or just me?"

Ophelia flinches at Ellis's quick movements; she teleports away from him, causing her to stumble into Nicholas. Her eyes move to Casey at the mention of his dream. That mixed with Ellis's comment could've meant nothing, but she still took it to heart and kept it in mind. She glances at Nicholas. "I need to talk to you" She mumbles.

"Uh—" Chase cuts in quickly. "—Whatever you have to say to him, you can say to us."

He stares down at her unconcerned how jumpy or fidgety she seems, or how her eyes dart around looking at the door and the window. He did notice how she grabbed Nicholas's hand, her thumb rubbing against his skin. "He's our brother first.

Whatever information you have for him is bound to come to us sooner or later."

Subconsciously Nicholas pulls Ophelia closer to him, their shoulders touching. He held her hand loosely, allowing her to stim in whatever way she needed. His stern gaze never left his brother. "No, we're not doing this." Before anyone could argue, he pulls Ophelia into a portal, now appearing in the kitchen with her.

Ophelia couldn't make eye contact with him, still squeezing his hand. "I meant to teleport home but I...I ended up in an office. It's the same one that I woke up in after I passed out during the mission. It all came back to me. White hair, black streak, called me a Time Bomb—" she rambles, swallowing hard. "—She wanted me to join her, said she needed me to help her with something. I refused then but, today when I appeared in that room again."

She pauses for a moment, her eyes squeezing shut. "She stood there with this sick grin on her face. Asked if I changed my mind, and when I told her no, she asked me how my siblings were and then left!" She lets go of his hand to run her fingers through her hair. "My siblings are gone—" Her voice broke as she met his eyes. "—I don't know where they are or what happened. It's just me and Cleo left."

"When did they go missing? Today?" His chests tightens and he steps closer, making sure to keep close. He allows her to keep rubbing his hand.

"Four of them were sent on a mission. It should've been quick! No more than four hours! But they didn't return. My Dad got worried and went to find them, but he came back empty-handed. Tyler took it into his own hands but didn't come back. The others were gone soon after." She could feel her stomach turn and her head pounding. "I don't know what to do," she whispers, her voice trembling. A tear slips down her cheek, and she quickly brushes it away, unwilling to let him see her breaking.

"We will get this figured out." Nicholas reassures her, putting a gentle hand on her shoulder. "You said you remember what she looks like, right? Maybe we can find something about her." He keeps his hand on her and teleports them to the library in the basement. "Preston had a book about all of the kids like us, the ones he calls OutKasts," he says walking down the aisles.

"He wanted to have as many of us as he could, for whatever reason," he mumbles "Maybe this woman will be in one of the books."

Ophelia sits down in a chair, eyes watching him carefully "This woman is older than us, like 30 or something. Preston didn't start adopting kids with powers until more recently."

Nicholas stops at a thick black book, carefully pulling it out. "It's possible that she was never adopted by Preston, that she's just some woman with powers. Either way, Preston kept a list of any known superhuman."

He flips through the pages until he got to the middle section of the book, there he found pictures of the people listed. They were always pictures taken secretly. A woman doing her laundry at a laundromat. A man eating at a restaurant. A couple walking their dog in the park.

There were also states scribbled down with an estimate of how many OutKasts were located there. Atlanta, Georgia, Arlington, Texas, York, Nebraska.

"Your dad is weird," Ophelia mumbles looking through the pictures labeled with names and their powers.

"Good thing he's not my bio dad," Nicholas muttered. He flips to a photo of a group. "Hey, that's your family."

Ophelia looked down at the photo, shoulders softening at the memory. Her mother had wanted a family photo, and so her father, ever willing to make his wife happy, had lined up all the kids in front of the house. This recent picture showed Ophelia at thirteen or fourteen years old.

"How did he get this?"

Nicholas just sighs and shakes his head. "The man is a mystery, a weird, mystery." He flips the page, a second family photo greeting him. He didn't remember this photo at all, he was young, maybe ten. He couldn't tell.

"Oh, baby Nicky," Ophelia coos, peering down at the only non-smiling boy in the photo. "There's Ellis, Casey, Karmin, Chase." She pauses, pointing to a young girl who stood off to the side, her hair in braids. Her hands intertwined together, resting against her stomach. She stared at the camera with a small smile. "Who's that?"

Nicholas pulls the book closer, studying the girl in the photo. “I have no idea. I…I have no memory of this photo even being taken.”

Ophelia takes the book from him and gently pulls the picture out of the laminated sheet it rests in. She flips over the card and read on the back. “The OutKast.” She reads. “June 8th, 2017. Rampage, Nightmare, Rogue, Phantom, Nexus, Freak.” She turns to him. “Who’s Freak? She has to be that girl, right?”

Nicholas stares ahead trying desperately to regain any memory of this event. He didn’t like not knowing. “Preston never called us anything but our code names. It was his wife who gave us names.” He pauses almost letting it slip that he had gotten adopted with his birth name, but that would require telling Ophelia about his origin story, and that he wasn't about to disclose.

Ophelia stares at the picture a bit closer, feeling a chill run down her spine. "Her smile," she whispers quietly, that sickly sweet smile burned into her mind. "That's her. That's the woman."

"How is that possible? You said she was a grown woman. In this picture she looks about the same age as us." Nicholas looks at her, noticing the fear and shock on her face.

"I don't know Nicholas! But I know that smile. I can't get it out of my head!" She points to the girl in the photo. "That's her."

Nicholas didn't look away from Ophelia's face. He didn't understand what was going on, but he hadn't seen Ophelia this shaken up before, so he trusted her. "Okay we will figure this out."

The library door slams open. "Ophelia!" Ellis gasps out of breath leaning against the door. "Cleo is here, says—" Before he could finish his sentence, Ophelia's younger sister stepped next to him.

"I think I know where the others are." She runs her fingers through her short strawberry blonde hair.

"How?" Nicholas asks skeptically, his eyebrow raising.

Cleo looks at him with narrow eyes. "Does that matter? I think I found some answers at this old building downtown."

Ophelia stands up waving her hand, brushing Nicholas off. "Well let's go, what are we waiting for?"

Nicholas opens his mouth to object, they knew next to nothing about this *Freak* and now all of the sudden her last remaining sister just happens to know where her siblings were. He didn't buy it, not even for a moment, but he looks into Ophelia's worried eyes, and he couldn't help but go against his better judgment. "Fine," he says standing up. "But we leave at the first sign of trouble."

The four of them, Ophelia, Cleo, Nicholas, and Ellis stand inside some old house where Cleo believed Freak was last seen. The house looms at the edge of town, its silhouette shadowed and jagged. Inside, the air is heavy with dust and the faint scent of mildew and decay. The floorboards groan under their cautious steps, as if the house itself were warning them to leave.

"Are you sure this is the right place, Cleo?" Ophelia asks softly, her eyes sweeping across what looked like the living room at the peeling wallpaper and cobwebs that stretched like veils across forgotten furniture. "It looks like no one has been here in ages"

"I don't know. It just *feels* right." Cleo whispers making her way up the staircase. The banister splintered, and each step let out an agonized creak as she ascends, her heart pounding louder than the noise.

They split up cautiously, Nicholas with Ophelia and Cleo with Ellis. In the parlor, Ellis brushes aside a curtain of cobwebs to reveal an old, dust-covered piano. His fingers hover over the keys but stops when Cleo clears her throat and shakes her head.

Upstairs, the others search the bedroom that smelled of mothballs and stale air. "Ophelia, I don't have a good feeling about this," Nicholas says seeing the empty room. "I know you want to find your siblings and I do too, but I don't think this is where they'll be."

Ophelia looks over at him with a small sigh. All Cleo had was just a *feeling* and they were taught never to base situations on feelings. But this was her sister, and Ophelia was so worried about her siblings that she couldn't think of anything else. "Okay," she says quietly, "Let's go."

"Hey Nick, it's almost dinner time and this house smell is ruining my appetite." Ellis calls from downstairs. "Can we go?"

Nicholas walks down the stairs, Ophelia following. "Yeah, there's nothing here." He walks towards the front door. "Let's go back home and figure out another plan."

"Leaving so soon?" A sweetly sickening voice rang out.

The four of them slowly turn around and were face to face with a woman with dark black hair and one white streak. Pale gray eyes, and an insincere smile. Ophelia knew it better than anyone. Freak.

Ophelia grabs Nicholas's hand, squeezing it hard, her eyes never leaving the woman. "What do you want." She spoke hoping her voice didn't betray her fake confidence.

"Well, you ignored my offer and then I took your siblings." She pauses. "But I realized you don't exactly know what I need from you, which is just rude, I don't want to be rude." Her eyes scan Ophelia before clicking her tongue against her teeth. "I'll just get straight to the point, you are a Time Bomb!"

Ophelia stares her down. "What?"

Freak starts to pace in a small circle while talking. "You ever get really upset and notice that the atmosphere has changed?"

Ophelia stays quiet, refusing to play along. Although, she couldn't help but think about how her dad mentioned something like that before. She remembers one time when she was younger Tyler kept teasing her, making her really angry and annoyed. Thomas had quickly intervened and sent them to their rooms. Ophelia remembers noticing it was snowing but it was in the middle of summer.

Freak smirks at her silence. "Exactly. As you get older your powers get stronger. When you feel upset or angry your element aspect alters the weather."

"So, what. You want to make her weak enough for her to, what, start a blizzard? Freeze over the town?" Ellis asks confused.

Freak shrugs, "Something like that." She looks around the dusty room and chuckles to herself. "I really let this place go. I never really liked living here, but it's a good place to plan revenge." She stops her pacing and looks at the group. "Wir werden gewinnen!" She snaps her fingers, and Cleo starts walking towards her.

The girl's hands were outstretched, her fingers splayed as tongues of fire curled around them like eager serpents. With a sharp exhale, she thrust one hand forward, and a stream of fire shoots out, arcing through the darkness to strike the walls around them. The flames roar to life, consuming everything they touch in a cascade of orange and gold.

"Well, this was fun!" Freak glances over at Nicholas. "Tell father I never forgave him for what he did." With that, she and Cleo disappear.

The building erupts into smoke and the flames roar around them, a cacophony of cracking wood and popping embers as smoke filled the air, heavy and choking. The three kids huddle together in the middle of the room, their wide eyes reflecting the flickering orange and red of the inferno.

Ophelia stands staring at where her sister had just been. Had Cleo just tricked her? Was this her plan the whole time? Did she know from the start that this place was just a trap or did Freak have her under some kind of control. She feels more lost and confused than ever. Freak had called her Time

Bomb, kidnapped her siblings and now she stood in this burning building of her sisters own doing.

"We have to go!" Nicholas yells, his voice cracking, barely audible over the roaring fire. He threw his arm up to shield his face from the heat as he tries to peer through the thick smoke, sweat dripped down his temples, and his shirt clung to his back, damp with fear.

He grabs Ophelia's arm before making a portal. "Ophelia! Come on!" He shouts before pushing the fear-stricken girl through the portal, waiting for Ellis to follow before he jumps through himself.

Chapter 14

Ophelia gasps and sits up quickly. She starts to catch her breath while looking around trying to figure out where she was.

It was the same office with white walls, a desk and a chair. She didn't remember passing out.

"Good morning, Time Bomb." That mocking, annoying voice spoke.

The girl looks at the chair where Freak sits. "Leave—Leave me alone." Her voice rough and hoarse, it hurt to speak.

"I need you, Time Bomb."

"Will you stop calling me Time Bomb?" She was starting to grow annoyed with her, and that name. "I am not helping you. I will get my siblings back."

Freak smirks lightly, “We will crush that light. You have that one weakness that will break.”

Ophelia stands up shakily still feeling weak from being in such a heated room for so long. “I will never join you.”

“Something... Or someone is your weakness,” she says in a taunting tone.

Ophelia ignores her, eyes closed, willing herself to wake up.

“They think you’re dangerous, Time Bomb,” she said, “Don’t you think it’s time to show them just how dangerous you are? Wir werden gewinnen.”

Chapter 15

Ophelia wakes up with a start, her eyes quickly scanning the room she was in, hoping she wasn't still in that office.

She starts to calm down noticing the bedroom eerily tidy, with no warmth or clutter. The walls were painted a muted gray, empty of any posters or photos, as if any trace of personality had never even existed. A single desk sat in the corner of the wall with neatly stacked books and a small notebook.

She looks down at the plain, dark sheets that covered her. She knew exactly whose room this was. The only bedroom where the bed had no extra pillows, no chair piled high with dirty laundry, and a small bookshelf against the wall with mainly history and science books.

Nicholas's room.

She must've passed out shortly after he had pushed her through the portal. She climbs out of the bed and quietly makes her way through the hallway. She stops at the top of the stairs hearing Nicholas's voice. Loud and angry.

"Tell us what you know old man!" Nicholas yells.

Preston stands in the middle of the room, his children and Thomas O'Connor surrounding him. "I know plenty of things Rogue," he says staring right through him.

"You know damn well what I mean!" Nicholas spits. "We met Freak. She said she would never forgive you for what you did. What did you do?"

"Ah, she always was the stubborn one."

"I don't understand. You had another kid? Someone else like us?" Ellis asked, "I mean, she looks older than us."

"She grew up with us," Nicholas says, his eyes never leaving Preston's face. "I saw her in that family photo you made us take when I was ten. She looked the same as me."

"She was eleven." He corrects.

Nicholas steps forward but stops when Casey grabs his arm. "We all know you're a bad father but come on, what did you do to get someone to act like this?"

Preston shoots a look at Casey. "I did good for what my purpose served, Nightmare. If anyone was the failed guardian, it was Thomas."

Thomas scoffs and looks at him. "All the children I adopted harbor no hate towards me. The only reason they are in danger is because of you."

Preston shrugs a bit. "But do they have all their memories?"

Thomas narrows his eyes as he stares at the man. "Don't start," he whispers, "Or maybe now would be the perfect chance to bring up Abigail." At that threat Preston went quiet but that did not get the attention off of Thomas.

Nicholas's head whips over to Thomas. "Whose memory did you erase?" His voice low, ready to lose his cool at any given moment.

"Ophelia's." Casey whispers softly, his eyes lowering until he could see his black shoes against the grey carpet.

The room grew silent as Ophelia made her way down the stairs. “What?” She whispers softly, her eyes trained on Thomas. “You did what?”

Thomas looks at her, startled, then his face changed to sadness, regret clouding his eyes. “Ophelia, I thought it was the right thing to do...”

“What did you take from me!” She yells.

Thomas stays quiet, looking down at the ground instead of his daughter.

“I can tell you,” Casey spoke quietly, only looking up to look at the girl on the staircase. “I read it in Preston’s notebook.”

Ophelia ignores the scoff that came from the older man. “What was it, Casey? Please. Tell me.”

He looks into her eyes and felt a lump forming in his throat. “Preston... He killed your parents," His voice falters, looking away from her. "Thomas kept that memory from you."

"What?" Her voice cracks.

"Ophelia, I did it to save you the pain that—" Thomas says.

"Show me." The girl demands, staring at Casey.

"What?" The boy asks confused.

"I know you can do dream and memory whatever," she says waving her hand around. "Do it. Bring it back. I want to remember."

"I don't think that's a good idea, Ophelia" Nicholas walks over to her but made no moves to reach out and touch her. "It will be too much."

Ophelia didn't look at him, her gaze locked on Casey. "Please, Casey. I know there has to be other memories of my parents besides the end. The world never gave me anything but reasons to be afraid, I just want one good memory of what I could have had."

Casey lets out a breath and nods. "Nicholas is right," he warns her, "It's going to feel overwhelming, so at any point please tell me when to stop."

Ophelia makes her way to the couch and sits down, nodding towards Casey.

Nightmare closes his eyes, his hands trembling slightly as they reach out. His touch was light but charged, fingertips brushing against the girl's temple. He didn't always need to come in contact with the individual for memory resurfacing, but he felt like he should this time around to comfort his friend.

A soft, iridescent glow began to shimmer around them, faint at first, then pulsing stronger.

For a moment, nothing happens, and then the flood gates open. The air grew heavy, like the weight of an impending storm, as the memory burst to the surface. It was raw and overwhelming, like a film reel spinning too fast, scenes overlapping in chaotic clarity. Ophelia gasps, her body jolting as an invisible blow strikes her.

She could see it clearly now. A young Ophelia on a stool in a cozy kitchen, a floral apron tied around her small frame. Her mom leaned over her shoulder, guiding her hands as they rolled out dough for cookies. As they baked together, her mom waved a hand over the cookie dough, and sparkles of red light danced above it. "You can never have too much sweetness," her mom whispered with a grin. The girl mimicked her movements, her tiny hands glowing faintly as she giggled.

The memory fades and another one sets in. A winter afternoon, her dad knelt beside her in the yard, a mischievous glint in his eye. With a wave of his hand, water droplets in the air froze into intricate shapes. “What should we make today?” He asked. She clapped her hands, her eyes lighting up. A delicate rose formed in her palms, its petals shimmering with frost. Together, they crafted a miniature ice kingdom, complete with frozen knights and sparkling towers.

Now before bed, her mom wove magical stories, conjuring faint images of the characters in the air above her bed. Princesses danced in shimmering gowns, dragons roared softly, and castles floated in glowing clouds. Sometimes

Ophelia added her touch, changing the color of the dragons' flames or making stars twinkle in the castle sky. Her dad would walk in, frost trailing from his fingers as he cooled the room just enough to make her cozy under her blankets.

She felt safe and comfortable.

In a clearing near their home, the family practiced their powers together. Her dad created icy obstacles, her mom conjured glowing orbs, and the girl darted between them, her hands sparking with a mix of magic and frost. "Focus, sweetheart," her dad said gently, guiding her movements. Her mom gave her a wink. "Or don't. Chaos can be fun, too."

The memory surges through Ophelia and Casey. Her face twists in pain as she could see and *feel* every second of it. She could see her mother's face clearly, feel her presence as if she was beside her.

Her presence, a soft breeze that made the world feel safe. She had long, dark hair, cascading in gentle waves, and her skin was a rich, warm brown that seemed to glow in the sunlight. When she spoke, her voice was smooth, like honey, coaxing the girl to be calm when the world outside felt too chaotic. Ophelia could remember a moment when she had been upset, tears staining her cheeks. Her mom had sat beside her on the edge of the bed, pulling her into a gentle hug, and whispered soft words of reassurance. A faint golden light shimmered around her, an aura of magic that made everything feel peaceful. Ophelia now basks in the moment of remembering how safe she felt, not just from the troubles of the world, but from the storm of emotions that raged within her.

Before she could get too comfortable with the memory of her mother, it fades away and now she could see her father.

His tall frame and broad shoulders made him seem formidable, but his presence felt steady and reliable. He had icy blue eyes that, though cold at first glance, held warmth for those he loved. His skin pale, almost porcelain, and his hair short and dark, a few silver strands peppering the sides of his temples. Ophelia could remember his soft smiles, rare but genuine.

He was the first one to pick her up when she tripped and scraped her knee. Without hesitation, he knelt beside her, his ice powers cooling the sting of the wound, soothing it almost immediately. His large hand gently cupped her chin as he examined the scrape. "You’re tougher than this," he murmured with a rare smile, before pulling her close for a quick hug. She remembered feeling that despite his quiet nature and distant appearance, he would always be there when she needed him most. He was like a snowstorm, still, unshakable, protective.

Ophelia cries out, clutching her chest as if trying to hold herself together against the onslaught of feelings. “No... Please.” She chokes, but the memory starts to fade away. She wasn’t ready to let them go.

When it finally ends, the glow around Casey fades, leaving him pale and trembling. He staggers back, his hands falling away as if burned. “I’m sorry,” he whispers, voice hollow.

Ophelia sits slumped and silent, tears streaming down her face. She stares at nothing for a moment before her eyes shift to Thomas who reaches out to comfort her but stops short. She then looks at Preston, his pale blue eyes looking at her with an almost bored detachment, slight smirk playing at his lips. He believed he was untouchable, unapproachable.

His face held no warmth, just a cold confidence that made it clear he believed himself above the rest.

"I could've had my parents, but you took that from me." She spoke refusing to let her voice shake. She would not give him that satisfaction.

"No." Preston states simply. "You were never meant to have this. You are dangerous."

Her icy blue eyes lock onto the man before her. With controlled breath, she summons the cold, her fingers crackling with frosty energy. She flicks her wrist, and sharp icicles shot from her palms, slicing through the air. But she didn't aim for him. Instead, the ice bolts flew just past his shoulder, embedding into the wall behind him with a loud, freezing crash.

Preston flinches, but the girl's expression remains unreadable, her face cold. She could have hit him, she was capable of it, but she didn't.

She tilts her head, watching the frozen shards shimmer, and then glances back at him, her lips curling into a faint, almost threatening smile. "I guess we'll just have to see how dangerous I can be to you then."

With that, she disappears into the pale purple light.

Chapter 16

The room stood in shock, staring at the icicles that were embedded in the wall behind Preston. Preston refused to stand there any longer after Ophelia tried to make a spectacle of him.

"Well." He states. "What a tantrum she threw, Rogue she's your little... Distraction," he says not even looking towards Nicholas. "You get this mess cleaned up" Preston starts to walk away but froze when the sound of someone's laughter filled the room.

It started low, quiet and amused, but quickly rose into something more unhinged, echoing off the walls with a chilling resonance.

Preston whips around finding himself face to face with the Freak's grinning face. "Hello Father."

Her figure appears in midair, shimmering with a glow that outlines every detail of her face and form. Light seems to weave through her image, casting faint ripples that dance along the edges like a reflection on water.

Nicholas's posture straightens at the sight of Freak in his living room. His dark eyes track the intruder with intensity, scanning every detail. He didn't move, didn't react, but his mind was already working ten steps ahead.

Karmin's jaw clenches at the scene with narrowed focus. With a sharp motion, she thrusts her hand forward, and the anger within her solidifying into a blade that shimmers a fiery glow. It was the perfect reflection of her rage towards her father for what he had done to her closest friend. Sharp, unyielding, dangerous.

"Oh no need to be afraid," Freak muses. "I am merely a hologram thanks to one of my little friends over here." She glances away towards someone that the group did not see, before turning back her gaze to focus on Preston. "Miss me?"

"A-Abigail." He whispers softly.

"Ah," Freak says sharply. "You never wanted to call me that name before. You lost your chance when you cast me aside." She hisses.

Chase steps up blocking a cowering Ellis, his eyes shifting from Freak to Preston. "Who is this, Dad?"

Preston opens his mouth, but nothing came from it. He just stares, eyes wide at the hologram in front of him.

"Spit it out old man!" Nicholas shouts.

"Oh, don't worry, I have no problem reliving our little tale," Freak said with a small smirk. "I am Preston's first daughter." She hums, "Isn't that, right?"

"He only had one daughter, Karmin," Chase said nodding his head to his sister whose stance never wavered.

"Only one *adopted* daughter," Freak tuts. "I'm Preston Peters' biological child. Connected by blood and nothing else." Her eyes narrow at her father.

Freak continues knowing that her father, always the coward, would not be the one to explain what was happening. "My mother brought me into this world and raised me as any mother would want to raise their daughters. Soft, kind, sweet, strong." Her hologram starts to pace the floor. "But Preston raised me to be hard, calculating. A weapon. He adopted you five and raised me alongside you. I was taught combat." She pauses, "That was until I became aware of my power, and my own strength."

"What's your power?" Karmin asks, Preston beating her to it.

"Manipulation."

Freak smirks. "Like father like daughter!" She waves her hand. "Anyway, when I started to realize I did not like how Preston was treating me or you guys, he tried to silence me. But I wouldn't go quietly." She steps in front of Preston, and even though she was not physically there, the older man flinches slightly, his eyes dropping to the floor. "You took me on a car ride." Her voice quiet. "Mom was with us. I thought we were finally having the family bonding moment I've always wanted. Like a normal family."

Though her voice was softer now, it still drips with anger. “We arrived at this forest, but it was oddly quiet. I remember not being able to hear anything, no birds, no animals, just the crunching of the leaves and sticks under our feet.” Her gaze stays hardened on Preston, but she looked as if she was reliving it. “He took us to this stone arch, overgrown with moss and ivy. I remembered how the stones glowed faintly, their surfaces had intricate carvings of symbols that seemed to shift. Before I could ask what we were doing, the archway began to shimmer. I could hear a faint hum, and light began to twist and ripple inside.”

“Abigail I—” Preston starts only to be cut off by Freak’s voice growing louder.

“He pushed me inside!” Her voice seems to shake the walls, Preston’s eyes lowering back to the floor. "I fell for what felt like eternity, I could hear my mother's screams." She looks at him, "What did you tell her? My mother. The woman you claim to love so much. What did you tell her you did to her only daughter? Her only child."

Preston didn't speak, he didn't look up at her. It was the one and only time the kids had seen him look so weak, cowardly, fragile. Any arrogance and confidence he had earlier was now stripped away.

She looks up at the group of kids she once considered her siblings. "I fell and passed out. Once I awoke, I wasn't in my timeline. I was in the past." She hums softly. "An elderly couple found me, took me in. Raised me as their own."

"I did not know where you would end up," Preston starts. "I read in books that that arch was a portal, never specifying where to. I just needed...

Abigail you were…" He sputters out, not being able to put his past actions into words. He needed her gone, but now that she was back, how could he explain that. He wasn't expecting to see her ever again.

"Why are you back?" Chase asks, his opinions on his once great father were now starting to fade from him.

Freak makes eye contact with him and grins. "While I was there, I learned about this group that the elderly couple despised. Perhaps you can recall them by name, father? Red Storm." She glanced at Preston, feeling delighted at how he squirmed at the name. "Yes, I was raised for a short while by none other than Arthur Peters."

"My grandfather," Preston whispers softly.

"Correct!" Freak says in mock cheerfulness. "From him I learned about this so-called Storm

Soul, the one who could cause destruction to the world if used properly." Her eyes flicker to Nicholas. "I call her Time Bomb."

Ophelia. Nicholas didn't flinch or make any sudden movement where Freak would realize that her words made him feel something. She was talking about *his* Ophelia, using her for mass destruction.

"Why?" Chase speaks up. "Why would you want to do something knowing you could end the world?"

Freak looks over at him, a small smirk growing on her face. "Simple. Preston wanted that child dead. Much like the rest of the super powered population. He despised you guys," she says looking at the group. "Hated me when he learned I was one in the same. He trained us to be prepared for this

Storm Soul. To destroy her, then he would simply dispose of us."

Preston could feel all eyes on him now. "Abigail you weren't meant to be like..."

"Like what?" Freak snaps. "Like one of them? I know how you felt when you realized your precious daughter had power running through her blood. You called me Freak," she hisses, "How did you feel when you realized I had to get my powers from someone? That it was mother?"

Preston opens his mouth but then goes quiet, his eyes glancing over to Thomas.

"You didn't" Thomas whispers. "I knew my memory gun went missing. I thought I had destroyed it, but you stole it didn't you?"

Preston looks up at the wall, still not meeting anyone else's eyes. "I loved Rose," he says quietly.

"It broke me to learn that she was one of them...After I... After Abigail, I erased Rose's memory of the incident. Of her ever even having powers." His voice slow, not as strong and commanding as it once was. "I created a device to contain her powers and reduce them over time," he chuckles slightly, "She was none the wiser, she *loved* that bracelet I gave her. Still, she refuses to take it off. Not that it would matter now, her powers almost desolate."

Chase stares blankly at the man he used to look up to, the man he used to follow so blindly, who he used to call father. "You never cared about anyone, did you?" His voice quiet. "You didn't care about us, about Abigail. Not even mom. Nothing was ever good enough for you. You betrayed your own daughter, your wife."

Casey spoke up, his voice filling with anger. “You used us as weapons towards each other. You even suppressed your own wife!” He stares coldly at Preston. He loved the woman he grew up calling his mother, she was the only one he ever had, knowing now that she had memories that were lost, hurt him. “All she ever did was love you. Even though you were a sick, twisted monster.”

At that, Preston’s eyes snap up to Nicholas’s. “No amount of love could ever change a monster.”

His voice sent chills up Nicholas’s spine, he reaches for the blade he kept holstered with him but stops at the sound of clicking heels on the hardwood floor above them.

“Preston?” Rose’s soft voice calls from the stairs, not yet rounding the corner to see them. “I was going to start dinner. Are the kids home?”

The soft voice of her mother made Abigail's heart stutter. She froze, fingers trembling. Her eyes fluttering shut, her breath hitching.

Beneath the armor, beneath the mask, she was just a girl. A girl who had lost her mother. A girl who *needed* her mother.

"Mother!" Abigail calls out, her voice weak and cracking. Tears well, burning at the edges of her vision, threatening to spill. For a moment, she was just a child again. Alone. Scared. Reaching out for the comfort she had been denied.

"Yes sweetheart?" Rose's voice trails from the hallway, still not yet reaching the top of the stairs. Confusion laced in her voice, not knowing which of her children were calling for her, just that one had needed her.

"Hush up." Preston whisper, voice straining. A quick flick of his wrist in the holograms form caused the projection to sputter and dim with a soft hum.

Freak's image wavers, the sharpness of her features blurring and distorting. "Please! It's me Momma, it's—!" Her wailing voice falters into a garbled mess of static, like a radio losing signal.

Preston's breath catches in his throat as the figure began to fade, until all that remains was the empty space where the hologram had once stood. He clears his throat, spinning to face his wife who now appears at the top of the stairs. "Nothing, my love," he says, confidence reappearing in his voice. "Now is the perfect time to start dinner, all the children are present."

Chapter 17

October 2016

Ellis runs down the stairs and slides into the living room, stopping at his mother's armchair. "Mom, can we have story time?"

Rose lays her sketchbook down, the drawing of a moonlit forest half-finished. "Of course, darling."

From his seat on the couch on the opposite side of the room, Preston's low voice speaks. "They do not need stories, Rose. They are not children."

"He is eight years old, Preston." Her voice is soft but firm.

Preston scoffs but does not look up from his heavy leatherbound book. "They are not normal children. They are not meant for the... frivolities you are so inclined to grant them." He looks up and stares at Ellis, his voice a low, final warning. "Go, Phantom. Cease this childish nonsense."

Ellis doesn't protest. He knows better. He quietly goes back upstairs, with less energy than he had coming down.

Rose sits still for a beat before slowly rising, setting her sketchbook on the end table. "I am going to retire for the night. Do not stay up too late."

On her way to her bedroom, she hears Nicholas's soft voice coming from his room.

"I'll love you during the bright mornings, and I'll love you during the dark nights."

Rose pushes open the door gently and sees all her children in Nicholas's room: Karmin and Casey snuggled in Nicholas's bed, while Chase and Ellis lie on the floor on a blanket pallet.

Nicholas must have heard the door open, because he instinctively hides the book under his blanket, his shoulders tense.

Rose says nothing as she shuts the door and takes a seat next to Nicholas. Always the caretaker, more than he would ever admit. Wordlessly, she holds her hand out for the book.

Nicholas hands over the book and crawls over to the empty blanket space next to Ellis.

The book is well-loved, a paperback with a faded cover and torn edges. It isn't something Rose has seen before. She opens it and reads the inscription in her head:

To my Darling Chase,

No matter how far away we are, you will always be my baby.

- Mum

Rose glances up at Chase, who isn't making eye contact with her. Her hands move back to the page, and she quietly starts to read aloud.

"I'll love you on the hottest of days and the coldest of nights. I'll love you when we laugh, and I'll love you when we fight." The soft rustle of the page is heard as she turns it. "I'll love you when you're tiny, and I'll love you when you're big. I'll love you forever and always."

Rose glances up and sees the children fast asleep, except Nicholas.

"Sleep, Nicholas," she whispers. "He will not do room checks tonight. I'll make sure of it."

Rose watches him close his eyes and stays there, sighing on the floor, the book hugged to her chest, watching their chests rise and fall as sleep claims them.

Chapter 18

Ophelia O'Connor lays on her back on the old, rusted brown car. The metal roof felt cold under her fingers, but it was not from her doing. For once, ice did not follow her unregulated emotions. She lay there, staring at the sky, numb, frozen.

The cool breeze and the smell of the fresh flowers from the field did nothing to shake the girl from her trance. Her mind floods with memories she forgot existed. Her mother's face, her laugh, her magic, the graceful powerful way she carried herself. Her father's cool and stable demeanor, how he always made her and her mother breakfast, teaching her about snow ice cream and making it during the winter months.

Her ballet recitals that her parents cheered her on at, always presenting flowers to her.

Sleepovers in the living room that consisted of blanket forts and junk food.

Tears well up in her eyes as the memory of her mother's laugh played on a loop in her head. Slowly, she lifts her hand, a faint, pale purple glow began to pulse around her fingertips. The air in front of her began to shimmer and in the growing light, a scene began to form.

A memory. Her memory unfolding in the air. The image solidified, becoming sharper, clearer, until she could see herself standing in a sunlit park, her parents beside her. She was younger, perhaps no older than eight, and her mother's hand was gently resting on her shoulder, she could hear her father's laughter.

The memory flickers, like the static of an old projector, and the soft purple light radiates from her, pooling around the image as if holding it together. The scene was vivid, her mother's soft voice, her father's teasing smile. The warmth of the moment was almost tangible, like it could pull her back into that time, back into the safety of those simpler days.

"You are my strong girl, Ophelia," her *mother whispered softly kissing the top of her head.*

"I'm not that strong," young Ophelia says lifting up her hands, the same pale purple light flickering from her fingertips. "I can't do my powers like you can."

"You are very strong, my love," her mother says. "If there is one thing, I want you to learn is that you are the only one who can tell you who to be."

The child thought for a moment. "I am Ophelia Aldane."

“Precisely.” Her father says rubbing her head, messing up her hair.

“Ophelia Aldane. My powerful storm,” her mother hummed. “Soft and strong.”

Ophelia looks at her mother confused. “The kids at school say you can’t be soft. If you are then you’re weak.”

“There is strength in softness.” Her mother told her. “It’s all about resilience. The courage to stay open, to remain gentle, and to still rise, no matter the pressure. No matter what others say.”

Young Ophelia was quiet for a moment mulling over her mother’s words.

For a moment, Ophelia let herself feel the memory that was playing out in front of her, really feel it. The comfort of her parents' love. The memory felt alive, she couldn’t take her eyes off of it, wishing to reach out and touch it, to be enveloped in her parents' arms, shielded with their love.

"Some kids at school say I'm dangerous." Young Ophelia spoke softly.

Helena Aldane's deep brown eyes turned to look into her daughters. "Prove them wrong."

There was strength in her voice that Ophelia could feel back then, and now even still.

The light began to flicker again, and the image wavered. Her eyes clench shut for a moment, willing herself to keep the memory playing to hold on as long as she could. Her hand tremble slightly as the memory starts to shake. The scene in the air around her blurs, the purple light flickering.

Her heart aches, longing for the time she couldn't get back.

The ache of knowing that she couldn't hold onto these memories for long twisted in her chest. No matter how much this memory reminded her that the world had not given her all bad things, she wouldn't be able to get back to it. It was fleeting.

The pale purple glow flickers one last time, the image slowly dissolving into the air, leaving only the faintest trace of light behind.

"I had an experience like that once." A voice startles her, causing her to sit up and quickly conjure an ice dagger. Only relaxing when she saw Nicholas.

"What are you doing here," she mutters, dissolving the weapon before scooting over so he could sit with her.

"You think I wasn't going to come check up on you?" He teleports next to her, putting his hand to his heart. "I'm hurt."

Ophelia rolls her eyes and lays back down. "I know you're here to put together some kind of game plan, but Nicholas. I don't know." Her voice was soft, wavering slightly like she was unsure of what to say next. "I just found out everything I thought I knew was a lie. On top of that my siblings are gone... and I just..."

Nicholas shakes his head. "I'm not here to talk strategy," he says simply. "At least not right now." He takes a deep breath, his back straightening, his hands on his knees. "I spoke with Thomas before I came."

"I don't want to hear anything from him." She scoffs.

"I asked why Thomas was there that night. With your parents," he says not looking at her. "He said he was there because your mother invited him. She told him she knew what was going to happen and that Thomas and his wife were the only people she could trust. Especially, after his experience with taking care of all the other adopted kids."

Ophelia looks at him. "You're telling me he knew that she knew what was going to happen?" Her eyes shift a bit. "But why didn't she try and stop it?"

"I asked the same question." He glances down at her. "The future is a fickle thing. It's going to do whatever it wants, however it needs to. Your mother was a smart woman, a strong witch, she knew she wouldn't be able to stop it."

Ophelia grew quiet for a moment thinking back to how scared her mother must've been knowing that her time with her daughter was limited. Did she know now that she was okay?

Hell, *was* she actually okay?

"Why are you telling me this?" The girl breathes out. "You don't even like Thomas that much, always suspicious of him. Worried he would be like Preston."

Nicholas hesitates for a moment, the words right there on his tongue but he couldn't quite speak them. "He isn't like Preston." He started, his eyes moving away from hers, clearing his throat before speaking. "You need him. I couldn't let you lose another important figure in your life if you didn't need to."

Ophelia could tell there was something the boy wasn't saying. Her eyes trail along the side of his face, and her mind drifting back to what he had first said when he got here.

"I had an experience like that once."

"What happened?" Ophelia asks.

He sits there for a moment, his posture rigid. The silence stretches between them. His expression remains cold, but his eyes, she could tell even just for a split second, flicker with something softer, something buried.

He clears his throat, the words he never allowed himself to speak swirling just beneath the surface. "I never wanted to talk about this again." His voice low and distant. His words felt unfamiliar to him. His hands, normally so steady, fidget with the material of his pants for a brief moment.

Ophelia swore she caught sight of his calculating demeanor momentarily slipping.

He hesitates again, sharing this part of himself felt...wrong. He was taught better than this. Trained better than this. He had never been one to share. Emotions and memories were things he'd always buried, to keep from being exploited as a weakness.

Unfortunately for him there was something about the girl sitting next to him. It made him question whether maybe just this once it was safe to let down his guard.

He took a shallow breath, then exhales it slowly. "I grew up in a place where..." He stops, the words threatening to choke him. His gaze flickers away, somewhere into the distance, as if searching for the right words, but all that came back was the raw memory.

A part of him wanted to stop, to lock it all away again, but another part, one he rarely listened to, urged him forward. “It wasn’t… easy,” he continued, quieter this time. “My father… My real father. Was a well-known villain. He never raised me to be like him. He *loved* me.” His eyes soften ever so slightly, but only for a moment. “He always made sure I stayed safe, far away from his work. He always fought for what was right, though that made him a villain. He taught me to be strong, taught me how to fight in case I ever needed it.”

His jaw tightens as the weight of the memories settles in. “Preston came to my father, told him that I would be safer with him. That all the people he had made enemies out of would find him, would hurt me,” he stops. “My father laughed in his face, told him he’d never give me up.” His eyes shift and now a voice in his head was screaming at him to be quiet, to stop. But he persisted. "Some people came after my father. They burned our house. Him and I weren't there but my mother..." His voice wavers, his eyes squeezing shut. "I was never able to prove that it was Preston's doing. My Dad never gave me directly to Preston, but that old man came for me in that god awful children's home."

"Preston thought that because of who my father was that I was a weapon of destruction. He made me this way." His voice returns to its hardened, cold stature. "I had to learn how to survive. To trust no one."

He looks at Ophelia. The one person who didn't need him to be perfect, who never showed any indication of wanting him to hide his past. And for once, it didn't feel like a weakness to let her see a piece of it.

"I angered Preston one day, and as punishment he made Casey pull out that memory of my house burning, my father breaking as he realized he lost his wife. Him leaving me," he mumbles, almost too quietly to hear. "But Thomas. Thomas isn't that way for you. He cares about you." He pauses briefly. "I care about you." The words sound almost foreign as they fall from his lips, but they were true. "I will always be here for you Ophelia."

A brief silence passes between them, the weight of his confession lingering, but for once he didn't regret it. Didn't feel the need to slip on his usual cold façade and abruptly leave.

Ophelia stays quiet, just taking in the moment and the meaning of his words. "Even though I am dangerous?" She whispers softly. "A Time Bomb?"

"I always thought there was beauty in chaos."

He smirks.

Chapter 19

Nicholas stands in his bedroom with his four siblings and Ophelia. His hands behind his back, staring at the people in front of him, commanding their attention without even needing to speak. "Alright. We need a plan to stop Freak," he said. "But before that we need to know if she said or did anything that stood out to you." His eyes shift to Ophelia. "Anything will help."

Ophelia starts thinking back to her interactions with Freak. "Oh, she kept saying 'Wir werden gewinnen' she said it every single time before she left."

Nicholas nods remembering hearing the woman say that before leaving the building with Cleo.

"What does that even mean?" Chase speaks.

Ophelia watches Nicholas glare at his brother before she continues to speak, "We Will Win."

"Huh?" Chase raises his eyebrow looking around the room hoping he wasn't the only one who didn't understand what that could mean.

"Chase, I don't have time for any of your moronic comments. Say something useful or shut up!" Nicholas snaps. He stands up making his way to his desk where he starts to shuffle papers.

"I found it interesting that Freak was sent back into time," Karmin says, her eyes pulling away from the argument that had just occurred between her two brothers. "She was eleven in 2017 and then time traveled and was found by Preston's grandfather. So, she ended up in the 30's?" Her eyes cast up at the ceiling as she thought meticulously about the words she thought before saying them. "She seemed really shaken when she heard her mother's voice."

"She seemed like she reverted back to a child," Casey agrees. "But her bodily age was closer to 30 years old."

Nicholas lifts his head, following the thought processes of his much more intelligent siblings. "Are you guys suggesting that Freak has the mentality of a 11-year-old?" He starts quickly writing his thoughts on paper. "Freak looked like she was 30 but acted, at certain times, like the age she was when she time traveled, 11 years old. This could be due to something I studied called "Split Aging" where time travel caused her body and mind to exist in different "timeframes." Her body aged to align with the time that passed in the real world, but her mind remained tied to the moment she first traveled," he speaks more to himself now.

Chase thinks for a moment, hesitating before speaking. "So, you're saying we're dealing with a villain with the mentality of a 11-year-old?"

Nicholas lifts his head, staring at the wall in front of him. "Wow, Chase actually got something right for once." He turns around, looking at the group then at Ophelia. "Is there anything else you remember?"

Ophelia thinks for a moment, her mind instantly drifting to her most recent interaction with Freak. "She said that I have a light... That she would crush. My weakness is someone or something."

It was Nichola's turn to be confused, but he didn't show it. Simply he mumbles under his breath while writing something down.

Ophelia couldn't help but notice Casey's face. Knowing the shocked, almost fearful expression well.

"Casey?" She spoke calmly.

"What. Nothing." He says quickly, shaking his head.

"If you know something, you need to tell us. It could possibly help us."

He chews on his lip, staying quiet for a moment "I-I know what she's talking about." His voice was barely above a whisper, "I had a dream of something that hasn't happened yet."

"So, you know Ophelia's weakness?" Nicholas asked.

Casey nods slowly avoiding eye contact with his brother. “I-I think so… But I can’t say. It could change the course of time. Man, sometimes the dreams don’t even happen or they’re in some kind of different context.”

“Useless!” Nicholas scoffs rolling his eyes.

Ophelia gives Casey a sympathetic smile. “I understand Casey, we will figure this out.”

“All we got so far is that Ophelia is being hunted by a 30-year-old woman with a mentality of an 11-year-old, who wants to find Ophelia’s weakness to destroy the world. All because her father tried to get rid of her.”

“And Freak has captured Ophelia’s siblings probably using them for her army.” Chase reminds him before pausing. “Maybe she has more OutKasts under her control.”

His face falls and he blinks “Thanks for that helpful insight. Chase.” Nicholas snaps sarcastically. He looks at Ophelia “Who would cause more of a threat out of your siblings? What are their weaknesses?”

“Megan and Cleo,” she said with a nod. “Megan has Animal Transmutation. Cleo has fire control,” her mind drifts back to the moment when Cleo had led them into that building just to burn it and leave with Freak.

“Weaknesses?” Nicholas asks again. He caught how her eyes shift down and he sighs gently, no frustration or malice in the air he let out. Not towards her, never to her. “Ophelia, there is a high chance Freak will be using them to get to you. If we know their weaknesses it will be easier to disarm them before they harm you.”

She shifts her weight before speaking slowly. "I don't know Megan's weakness. The twins, Elora and Alina have telekinesis, but they aren't a threat if they aren't by each other, powers don't work if they are separated." She takes a moment and thinks through all her siblings and their powers. "Just leave Cleo's weakness to me."

Nicholas nods. "Affirmative." He turns his focus to his siblings. "This is what the old man has been training us for. To prevent the extinction of our world. We must keep Ophelia protected, Freak is not to go anywhere near her, and no one under any circumstances should do fatal harm to any of the O'Connors." He orders. "Any civilians that happen to get caught in the crossfire, make sure we move them to a safe place."

He grew increasingly frustrated by not knowing when or where Freak would attack. All he knew was he had a lot of people he needed to keep safe.

Ophelia steps next to him. “I might be able to put a forcefield around where the fight is happening, to contain any chaos from spreading further.” This was one of the things she learned quickly, to use her magic to clean up any messes as well as prevent them if she could.

“As far as we know Freak has no weaknesses,” Chase interjects. “She bleeds just like the rest of us.”

“I don’t know if we should jump straight to that route, Chase,” Karmin says looking at him. “Yes, what she’s planning is awful, but she’s also only eleven.”

Suddenly, there was a deafening bang, like an explosion tearing through the air, causing the entire house to tremble violently. The walls groan under the force as shelves rattle and a fine layer of dust drifts down from the ceiling.

"We don't have time for a moral quandary over whether to take Freak's life or let her live, Karmin. She's here." Nicholas was now more alert. He opens a portal, quickly ushering his siblings outside.

The sky grew dark from smoke, multiple buildings collapsed releasing debris into the air. In the distance there were cars being tossed in the air, hordes of animals: tigers, lions, wild monkeys, and gorillas rampaging the city helping with the destruction. People who were trying to escape the mass of chaos were hit with a white light and turned into big, wild animals.

"Megan?" Ophelia wonders out loud, eyes scanning the mayhem in front of her, trying hard to find her sister.

Her eyes eventually land on her sister, but her demeanor had changed. Her normal blonde curly hair was now dark black with white streaks. Megan turns and looks at her. The girl's eyes were black and almost lifeless, then she turns around and walks back to where the animals had gathered in a line.

Slowly Ophelia could make out a group of people who were falling in line with the destruction. All of them were kids all chanting "Wir werden gewinnen." In front of the group stood Freak with her sick smile.

She waved lightly. "Hello, my Time Bomb."

Chapter 20

"Guys... Please tell me this is some kind of dream," Casey whispers eyes glued to Freak and her army of OutKast children.

"Lovely to see you again Time Bomb!" Freak says walking closer to the group. Her army of children and animals stayed back. "Want to join us now?"

Ophelia shakes her head, her eyes narrowing at the woman in front of her. Other times, back in that office, she would've been afraid. But not now. "Never."

She laughs "Oh, Time Bomb you think you can win with him?" She points to Casey who then looked offended. "Oh no! He'll give me nightmares," she feigns fear with a grin.

Ophelia doesn't say anything, Casey was stronger than he appeared. Besides, never correct your enemy when she's making a mistake. Instead, she glances over at Nicholas who was scanning the army, more than likely already coming up with a plan.

"Since I am so confident that we will win, I will spare you one of mine to make up for that." She nods towards Casey. The Freak turns back to her army and hums softly "Ollie." Ophelia's brother walked over to her. Freak whispers something in his ear and then shoves him forwards, where he falls right in front of the other group.

Ophelia quickly moves over to her brother "Ollie? Are you okay?"

It took a moment, but Ollie sat up. His eyes had gone back to their normal green color and his hair starts to fade from the black and white back to its normal dark shade.

"I'll give you a minute to prepare," Freak says, walking back to her army.

"Well, for a villain she's pretty nice," Chase says, helping up Ollie.

"Oh yeah, if you overlook the whole kidnapping and ending the world, she's a real peach." Nicholas snaps glaring at his brother.

"Okay guys we aren't going to get anywhere arguing like this. We have to work as a team." Ophelia cringed, ignoring how she sounded like some really bad cheesy movie about friendship, and instead she turns to Ollie "Is there anything you can tell us about Freak? Anything we can use?"

Ollie's voice came out hoarse as if he hadn't spoken in weeks. "She has everyone under her power, manipulation. It can only be broken if she's the one to do it."

"What if we just killed her?" Nicholas says simply.

Ollie looks at him, shocked by his brash plan. "That would work but the only problem is, she's too powerful to be killed like any normal person. It has to be a powerful enough source," he clears his throat before continuing. "Her power has grown stronger since she has technically been alive a lot longer than us. Truly her only weakness would be someone so pure and focused that they couldn't be twisted or corrupted by manipulation. Or some type of opposing force. An opposite force that cancels out her abilities could possibly render her vulnerable."

The group was quiet for a moment before Ellis spoke up. "Ophelia can do it."

All eyes turn to him

"I'm sorry, Ellis, but can you go and be stupid somewhere else?" Irritation drips from Nicholas's tone.

"What are you talking about Ellis?" Ophelia ignores his comment.

Ellis hesitates, his eyes shifting between her and the empty space next to her. "You are the power source," he whispers softly, almost like he was afraid to speak.

"Okay, if that's true then what do we do?"

Ellis's face went blank "I-I don't know."

"Of course you don't!" Nicholas exclaims with a tired laugh, "Useless."

"How come you don't know?" Her voice only ever being calm, not wanting Ellis to get frustrated and not talk.

Ellis's eyes shift between Ophelia and that empty space again. "She won't tell me, I mean she's trying to, but I can't hear her."

"Who? Ellis? Who is talking to you?" She studies his face before a shiver went down her spine. "You can see my mother? Can't you?" When the boy nods Ophelia steps forward and puts her hand on his shoulder. "Close your eyes Ellis, take a moment and focus on her. Nothing else just her."

"What if we moved Ellis to a safe place where he can focus on speaking to your mom?" Chase asks, noticing how Freak seemed to be growing impatient now.

"Great my team is full of geniuses," Nicholas mutters.

Ophelia was growing rather frustrated with his attitude. So, she shoots an ice pellet at his head. "Look, I know this is stressful and you're scared, we all are, but you don't need to be a jerk about it."

He looks at her for a moment before nodding softly.

"Okay." She looks at Ellis "Will that help you?"

He nods. "Yes, but I don't see how I can focus in the middle of a war."

"I can help," she says. "I'll create you a forcefield, I've been trained to use multiple powers at a time. I'll be able to keep you safe and help out over here."

Her attention then focused back to the others "We have to get to Freak and fend off the OutKast and the citizens that were turned into animals without hurting them."

"Knocking them out will work," Ollie says with a nod. "It won't kill them, nor will it revert them, but it will limit the amount of people after us."

"Times up Time Bomb." Freak calls, smiling.

Ophelia looks at her then glances at Ellis nodding to him to get somewhere safe. Once he was gone, she flicks her wrist focusing on putting a force field around him.

"One more chance, Time Bomb. Join us."

She shakes her head "You really can't take no for an answer can you?

"Very well. Wir werden gewinnen!" She yells to her army.

"Wir werden gewinnen! Wir werden gewinnen!" The kids chant back.

Soon the kids charge towards the group, the animals move over to Freak, protecting her.

"Great." Ophelia mumbles and quickly got to work casting a force field within a 500 foot radius, keeping the chaos from spreading throughout the city.

A girl barrels towards her, trying to land a punch. Ophelia ducks and shoots ice at her feet trapping her, and just before she could run off to go help Nicholas, or anyone else on her team, she heard ice cracking. Ophelia turns around and saw that the girl had grown 50 feet tall.

"Oh geez..." She mumbles. "I bet you're fun at parties." She runs away from the girl's giant feet as she tried to smash Ophelia like a bug. Her mind sifting through her years of training but surprisingly nothing had prepared her for a giant human. Her feet hit the pavement under her in a rhythmic thud, and she suddenly became more aware of the ice coursing through her body.

She focuses on it and soon each time her feet hit the ground, ice would spread rapidly. She kept doing this until she heard a loud thud and the ground shook. She didn't need to turn around to know the giant had fallen, quickly she teleports to a building that laid on its side from the earlier impact. Now standing at a good height above the giant, Ophelia got to work trapping the knocked-out giant in ice.

"That'll hold," she spoke proudly to herself before teleporting back to the ground. As soon as she landed, she was caught in a whirlwind. Dirt and dust clouding her vision, but it didn't take long to guess that her brother, Tyler, was running circles around her. Literally.

She tried to shoot ice out at him, but it missed and ended up ricocheting off the energy he gave and bounded right back to her. It was getting hard to breathe, it was hard to focus her energy on teleporting away.

"Okay, Energizer Bunny, that's enough." She could hear someone say. Then her brother fell down with a thud.

Ophelia slowly opens her eyes to see Nicholas with some kind of pole or something.

"Relax, it's a pool stick that I grabbed from what's left of our living room. He'll be fine but it'll buy us some time."

Ophelia nods gratefully while she caught her breath. “How’s Ellis...”

Nicholas’s facial expression changes to an emotion she couldn’t quite understand but he was quick to hide it, “I think he’s ready to talk with you. Make it fast.” And with that he teleported away.

Ophelia doesn’t give herself a moment to ponder what was going through his head. She teleports over to the area Ellis was hiding in. “Okay Ellis. What do you got for me?” She waves her hand taking down the forcefield.

“You are the opposing force that Ollie was talking about,” Ellis says after shaking off the shock of Ophelia just appearing next to him. “Freak relies on structure and absolute order, everything she has planned is all detailed.”

Ophelia's mind drifts back to the eerie way Freak's office had been set up, the way she spoke and how she moved. This was making sense. "Okay so what does that have to do with it?"

"You have chaos magic, Ophelia," Ellis said. "You *are* the chaos. You are what we need to weaken her power."

Her eyes shift while she processed his words. "So, what do I have to do?" She was having a hard time grasping how her magic could override Freak's manipulation.

"I don't know." He says sadly. "All your mother kept repeating was "You are a powerful storm" and "Prove them wrong" That's it, she wouldn't give me anything else."

Ophelia frowns slightly, hearing those words before but having no idea what they could mean.

“Okay,” she whispers softly, her power now glowing in her hands, teleporting herself in the middle of the chaos.

Ivy O’Connor stands still, her eyes narrowing as she feels the ground tremble beneath her feet. Roots begin to shift, breaking through the concrete, vines crawling up buildings, ready to attack. Karmin clenches her fists, focusing inward as a surge of anxiety builds in her chest. She lets the emotion spill out of her, turning it into a shield of worry, just as a thorny vine shoots toward her. The shield absorbs the impact, but the vines are relentless, continuing to snake toward her.

Karmin focuses on her anger, allowing it to grow inside her. The emotion solidifies into a massive blade of fiery energy that she swings to slice through the vines. The blade cuts through several thick tendrils.

Ivy stands with calm control, a small smile on her lips as she effortlessly commands the plants to push forward.

Karmin channels a surge of frustration conjuring into a wall that blocks the incoming attack. The vines smash against the wall.

The girl couldn't help but think of Ophelia and what her father had done, what he had done to Abigail, what Abigail had in return done to these other OutKasts. She could feel something starting to bubble into a solid mass of dark energy. This new weapon felt almost too heavy for her to manage, but she throws it toward Ivy. The mass of sadness crashes into the plants, the orb washing over Ivy in the process.

Ivy freezes, eyes blinking. “I’m... sorry.” She whispers as her eyes return back to normal before blacking out.

Nicholas stands calm. His eyes scan his opponent, this unknown OutKast, calculating every potential move. It wasn’t an O’Connor, so he was less inclined to care how the kid ended up after this fight.

With a flicker, he vanishes, only to reappear inches away from his opponent. A brutal kick connects, but he’s already gone again, his figure flickering in and out of existence

The blonde haired OutKast, a fighter with equal skill in hand-to-hand combat, seems fast, precise, and aggressive. His punches slice through the air, cutting with practiced ease but each time, the raven-haired boy vanishes just before contact, leaving him to punch empty air.

Nicholas couldn't help smiling at the frustration building in his opponent. "It's like you're not even trying." He teleports behind the OutKast, a striking jab to the ribs, a quick punch to the temple, and before he could react, Nicholas is gone again, he knows the laws of space and time are not in control of him.

Finally, winded and tired, the OutKast boy misses a punch as Nicholas appears behind him once more. This time, there's no hesitation. The fight ends in a blur, a flash of movement, a sharp blow to the back, and the battle is over.

Nicholas looks down at his fallen opponent, an unsettling grin on his face. It wasn't a fight for him, purely strategy, a calculation. And it was won before it even began.

Ophelia stands in the middle of the battlefield staring at the hoard of animals that surround Freak. She knew she could fight the animals as they came at her in droves. She also knew that's what Freak wanted, what she counted on. Ophelia simply opens a portal for the animals to fall in and opens another one, watching them fall infinitely, throwing Freak off her rhythm.

Freak's smirk fades slightly before it regains its regular place on her face. "You have no emotional attachment to these things. That's fair." She nods her head and Cleo steps out in front of her.

"I found your light," Freak sings tauntingly. "Your weakness. Fire." Her gaze trails to the red head. "Make her lose control."

Ophelia stands, her expression hardened, frost clinging to her fingertips as she raises her hands, sending a blizzard-like gust toward her sister. Sharp shards of ice shoot from the ground, forming walls and barriers in a desperate attempt to contain the firestorm before her.

Cleo's body enveloped in flames, responds with a burst of heat, melting the ice barriers as if they were nothing more than snowflakes. Fire erupts from her palms, trailing in arcs of flame, crackling and hissing as it collides with the cold around them.

"You've never been strong enough!" She yells. The flames intensify as she steps forward, each movement deliberate, the heat from her body radiating outward.

Ophelia stands firm, her gaze unyielding. She responds with a series of icy blasts, the cold cutting through the heat like a blade. But she can see her sister pushing forward, the fire growing stronger, the air thickening with the oppressive heat.

Suddenly, her sister moves faster than Ophelia had anticipated, closing the gap between them. She leaps, seizing her sister in a fiery embrace, her hands pressing against her shoulders, trying to melt the ice that coursed through her sister's veins. "I can't let you win." She hisses, her breath hot against Ophelia's neck.

She grits her teeth, her own hands freezing against her sister's skin, locking them both in an intense battle of wills. The air between them grows thicker, the fire pushes against the cold, but Ophelia digs in. With a grunt, she focuses her power into a final surge of ice, freezing the air between them. The temperature drops so rapidly that the flames around Cleo begin to sputter, then slow, then freeze in place.

Cleo gasps, her face paling as the icy grip of her sister's power takes hold. She pulls back, struggling, but the frost is relentless. Her flames sputter out, her body shaking with the cold that invades her every movement. She attempts to fight back, but the effort is draining, the cold stealing her strength.

Cleo meets her sister's eyes, for a split moment Ophelia could see the green return to them before her body went limp in her arms. Ophelia carries her away from the battlefield knowing she just needed a safe place to rest from exhaustion.

"I'm sorry," Ophelia whispers. She turns around ready to turn all of her energy loose on Freak, angry at having to disarm her sister. But she was met with familiar green eyes.

"Nicky?" Ophelia asks slightly startled, head cocking to the side. "Are you okay?" She scans his body for any major wounds but came up empty.

"You know I am never wrong, Ophelia," Nicholas starts. "I would really rather not admit that my factious brother was right, but I've been considering the facts. Your first solo mission with us and all of a sudden you have this urgent message? She called you Time Bomb, the same as what's written in the book."

Ophelia's eyes study his face, taken back. "Nicholas. We don't have time for this. What are you talking about?"

He blinks and tilts his head. "You only decided to help us when your family got roped up into all of this." He watches her. "I should've seen it sooner, but I was distracted. You *are* dangerous Ophelia. No matter which way you spin it. You were always destined to hurt us."

Chapter 21

The destruction around her was beautiful, the air thick with smoke, the ground cracked and scorched, echoes of destruction reverberating through the streets. Yet, amidst it all, she walks with a calm composure, her footsteps deliberate and precise.

Her heels click sharply against the concrete, each step methodical, as if she's savoring the moment. Her signature sick grin on her lips, her cold and calculating eyes, sweeping over the devastation she's caused, it was all just another piece of the plan she set in motion, and she knows it's almost complete.

Once she was satisfied with leaving a distracted Ophelia to fight her sister, she went to her next target. Her body seems to glide rather than walk, her posture straight and unyielding. She sees him, arm lifted ready to land another blow to his opponent. She grabs his wrist yanking him to look at her.

"AhAh Rogue. I have something much more exciting for you." Freak smirks down at Nicholas. She lets him rip away from her grasp, not needing to contain him.

"Tell me one reason I shouldn't kill you right now." He glares, his hand reaching for his blade.

"Oh." She tuts, with a fake pout. "We both know you couldn't kill me." Her smirk returns to her face, her head tilting slightly. "I tried to be the nice guy, I really did, I didn't want anyone to get hurt. She didn't even budge when I took her siblings as pawns." Her eyes studies the villain's kid she once called her brother. "But that little... Time Bomb, was not easy to work with." Irritation spewing through gritted teeth at the nickname.

Nicholas kept his guard up, jaw clenching and his fists tight. He listens carefully, keeping his snarky remarks for when he had enough information to be sure of himself.

"Nothing was breaking her until I realized, all that poor girl wanted was to not be seen as dangerous, and then she stumbled upon the one person who didn't see her that way. Who was that?" She taps her chin and suddenly next to her appeared an illusion of Nicholas. Cold. Calculating. "You like that? It's a new little power I picked up. You were the fuse for the bomb this whole time."

The illusion was threatening but he didn't believe Ophelia would fall for it if he could reach her first. "She won't fall for it. You're wasting your time."

Freak tilts her head up and raises her arms up in the air. "Any moment now I'll feel the sweet, cold, taste of victory." She started to walk past him. "Should've dressed warmer, it's about to get a little chilly... Auf Wiedersehen!" Her heels echoed sharply against the concrete as she left the boy alone.

Ophelia stands there, the illusion gone, the ground she stood on covered in a thick sheet of ice. All of it, Chase being against her from day one, the capturing of her siblings, regaining her memory, all of it was too much for her.

The words that the illusion of Nicholas spoke rang in her head.

"We were never meant to be. We were just killing time."

When Nicholas got there, he stood in front of her noticing the blue grey color of her eyes was gone, instead they were white. He watches her stare at him for a moment until Freak arrived, and she opened a portal taking them to the flower field.

Freak smirks seeing Nicholas appearing on his own just a few feet from them. “You really underestimated just how much you meant to her.” She sucks air in through her teeth. “Which is why this next part is going to hurt.” She looks at Ophelia. “I know what she’s capable of, but apparently betrayal wasn’t the thing that would send her over the edge. There’s simply only one thing that would really prove to her how dangerous she really is.” She glances at Nicholas. “Get rid of him Time Bomb. He’s no longer part of my plan.” She steps through the portal that led back to her destroyed city.

Nicholas still felt unsettled by the scene before him. Senses heightened by the absence of what he knew to be Ophelia. Had he really overestimated her? This might've been the first time he genuinely felt fear for another person.

Why did he have to fall for her?

Wordlessly Ophelia conjures up an ice blade, her eyes staying locked on his.

His gaze stays locked on hers, he could feel danger coming yet this hadn't stopped him from pressing on. “Ophelia this isn't—” His words were cut short by a sharp pain in his stomach. His eyes flicker down to the source of the hurt, finding the tip of the blade lodged into him. She had teleported to him while he was talking, no remorse, no mercy.

His body shook, a shaky gasp leaving him as he steps back. Crimson liquid soon began to leak through the fabric of his shirt. The warmth of his blood against his own skin made his body feel much cooler. A light trail of blood dribbles down the corner of his mouth as he stumbles back.

The physical pain wasn't as harmful as the emotional betrayal he felt. The look of disgust and disappointment displayed on his features accompanied by the evident expression of agony. "Ophelia..." He breathes out quietly.

Ophelia blinks and seemed to take a deep breath. Freak had released her hold on her, though she wasn't sure why. She looked at the knife in her hand and then over at Nicholas. "No-No Nicholas!" She teleports to him, catching him as he sways and before he hits the ground. She kneels down, resting his head in her lap. "I am so sorry!" She chokes out.

Tears forming in her eyes, her hand gently moving hair from his face. A burning sensation grew in her chest, it was uncomfortable and overwhelming. It hurt. And she starts to cry harder.

Unaware now that as she sobs the temperature got lower. It starts to snow rapidly and the ground below her turned to ice.

“Ophelia!” A voice calls. Ellis steps through the portal with his other siblings, his hand trying to shield his face from the winter snow.

“Help him!” She cries out to Ellis through tears “Please! Please help him!” Ophelia stands up when Chase picks up his brother. She quickly leads them to an old house that was abandoned in the flower field.

She watches Chase lay Nicholas down on an old dusty couch. She squeezes her eyes tightly shut before disappearing to find Freak. She found herself back where she had been fighting her sister moments ago.

"Well done Time Bomb!" The sinister voice speaks.

Ophelia lunges forward, blade ready in hand. Only for the blade to bounce off an invisible force and shatter.

Freak smirks. "Your mind was not strong enough against my manipulation. You can't kill me," she says.

Her eyes narrow with fury, hands shaking as she hurls a blast of ice at the woman. But the figure standing before her is unmoved, like the world itself is bending to her will. Her ice shatters harmlessly against an invisible barrier, the sound of it cracking like thunder in the silence.

She grits her teeth, refusing to back down. Her entire body tense with effort, her powers draining her faster than she can summon them. But she won't stop. She can't stop. Anger surges through her. That awful nickname echoes in her mind, the feeling of being powerless, the state she left Nicholas in. Being nothing more than a pawn.

Another blast of ice. This one thicker, more forceful. But again, it's absorbed by the same unseen wall, leaving nothing but a bitter sting of cold in the air. She takes a step forward, her face flushed with the strain of it all, her hands trembling violently, but still, she summons more ice, more power. The ground around her now becoming a sheet of frost, shards of ice littering the floor, but her opponent is still untouched, unfazed.

“Why do you still fight against me?” Freak asks in a rather bored tone. “We both went through the same thing. Both uncontrollable, both losing our mothers as punishment.”

Ophelia’s chest heaves as she gasps for breath, the frustration of Freak comparing their situations, the rage of having only proved everyone else right. She was a danger, and it fuels her.

It doesn’t matter how weak she’s becoming, how much it hurts. One more blast. This one will work. It has to.

But again, it’s absorbed, harmless. She stumbles forward on the verge of collapsing.

She won’t stop. Not until she’s proven herself.

Freak tilts her head at Ophelia, grinning at her weakened state. “You really think they will take you back after this? Nicholas is dead. His siblings know you're the reason. Everyone else knows you're responsible for this sudden winter. They know what had been true all along. You're dangerous."

Ophelia closes her eyes, her breathing heavy as she tries to think, tries to focus. An image of her mother's face appears, she didn't speak, a simple nod and the image was gone.

"So, I'll ask one more time. Why do you still fight against me?"

Ophelia lifts her head, straightens her posture, and stares directly in Freaks' eyes. Her hands conjuring another ice blade. "Because" she says taking a breath. "I am Ophelia Aldane. I refuse to let anyone else write my story." She plunges the knife deep into her skin.

Chapter 22

It wasn't easy to wound Nicholas. The raven-haired male often proved to be as cunning as ever, but his soft spot for Ophelia was his downfall. A stab wound to his middle was something he would survive, it would take more than that to send him to the other side.

However, anger was something that usually fueled him to press on, anger that he was currently lacking. In its place deep despair and heartbreak. These feelings surely slowed his progress.

Ellis got to work and was able to prevent the bleeding from pressing on. He knew enough about wounds, he and his siblings were trained to.

Chase hesitates for a split second before speaking. "So, this weather is from Ophelia, right?"

He glances around the room. "That means there's only one way to get the weather back to normal."

"Absolutely not!" Karmin interjects. "She was being controlled by Freak. There has got to be another way."

Chase shakes his head. "The only way to get rid of this weather is to take out the source."

"No! We are not doing that!" Karmin shouts.

Ellis was leaning over his brother who was slowly coming too. "Hey buddy," he coos softly. "Unkillable Rogue."

Casey glances out the window. "Uh guys?"

"I would just like to say I was right the whole time about her," Chase says smugly.

"Yeah, because your mind is so weak Freak definitely manipulated you!" Karmin shoots back.

"Guys!" Casey yells again pointing to the window. "It's not snowing anymore." His voice went quiet seeing Nicholas sit up.

Nicholas notices the change in the temperature immediately. He *knew* something wasn't right. The adrenaline surging through him was enough to make him forget about his injury.

Without a word he teleports to Ophelia.

That's when he found her.

Ophelia was kneeling down on the ground, feeling the impact. Her hand still grasping the ice knife she had used to pierce her own skin.

The snow stopped falling around her. She closed her eyes, twisting the blade a bit before pulling it out. She saw a pale green flash before she fell back. Her mind racing with thoughts of how everyone was right about her.

Chase, Preston, that book. All of it. Even her father, who always made sure to keep her emotions in check, he knew.

Nicholas drops to his knees, scanning her body. Unable to comprehend what he was seeing in front of him. His expression drops entirely, he choked out a sob.

"You know..." Ophelia spoke softly. "I liked the idea that I could do whatever I wanted with my life. A schoolteacher, work in a bookstore. That no one had control over my destiny but me. A shame I turned out this way, that I hurt you, almost hurt everyone else." She stares up at the sky while she spoke before turning her head to look at him.

The soft sound of her voice causes him to turn his attention to her. Red rimmed green eyes flicking to where she rested. He was crumbling, it shows in his clenched jaw, and tense shoulders pointing to the sky. He held her in his arms, holding her close.

Nicholas never cried, but he was past his breaking point. His eyes search hers, hardly able to breathe in her presence. He rather she used his breath instead of using it for himself. His hands found her wound, pressing firmly to the area.

"Ophelia—" He gasps out in another choked sob. "Ophelia stop talking. Save your breath." He ordered, but she pursued on.

She wasn't surprised to see him alive, very grateful that he was. But angry at herself. "You deserve so much more than the cards you were dealt with... please don't close yourself back off." She didn't want him to be angry at the world for something she had done.

Carefully, she moves her hand resting it on his knee. Her breathing slows more. "Promise me that you'll be selfish just once. You run around trying to save everyone but yourself." Her stupid, selfless boy overworked himself daily, unable to count the number of times she had to physically drag him away from whatever he was working on before he made himself sick.

It hurt so much that she had ruined everything, being taught at a young age to be careful, that her powers were strong, and she needed to be cautious. She didn't let that stop her from living life, she didn't become closed off. She found hobbies, made friends.

Fell in love.

But she ruined it all. She was weak. She didn't deserve him. Preston was right, she didn't deserve anything good because she was a danger. Those were the cards she was dealt.

He shakes his head. What she was asking was beyond him, especially now. “No. No you can’t leave me—” His voice rises. Tears fluidly streaming into multiple lines over his red cheeks.

The ice around her was melting faster now, and she grew more tired. She looked at him with a small smile, not wanting him to see her so sad before she left. “I guess this wasn’t the reality where I deserved a long life with you but somewhere out there is that reality… Where I get to wake up every day next to you… Where I deserve to be with you.”

Her voice was soft, her eyes closing. The sun shining down on her, the ice now completely melted. It was warm again.

“I love…” She murmurs softly. Her breathing stopped.

But the world kept going. People left their houses, children played, people went to work. The OutKasts, now shaken from Freaks hold, started the cleanup.

The world kept turning almost like two kids in love weren’t tested by the universe.

Almost like they hadn’t lost. Almost like nothing happened.

The second she took her last breath, his expression completely changed. A slight shake of her shoulders and his finger moving quickly to press against her neck. Two fingers measuring for a pulse.

Nothing.

At the discovery he felt his heart shatter. Leaving him nothing more than a hollow shell. He laid her down gently in her original resting position. Consumed by anger he grabbed the blade. His jaw set and he stood.

No words were said at her death. He remained completely silent.

He turns from her, teleporting quickly back to the house where his siblings were.

Glaring daggers at Ellis whom he immediately attacked. Running up towards his brother to push him against the wall. Gripping him by the collar of his shirt, the dagger's blade positioned in front of his neck.

Nicholas was unhinged, that was obvious. His actions were illogical, purely emotional.

"Bring. Her. *Back*." He growls lowly.

"Jesus!" Ellis screeches, only having time to see a blur of green before colliding into the wall.

There he could see the intensity in his brother's eyes. He stays frozen feeling the blade against his neck.

The room erupts with surprised shouts and protests.

"Rogue! What the hell!" Chase yells.

"Nicholas what are you doing?!" Casey shouts.

"Put it down Nicholas." Karmin pleads.

Ellis stares wide eyed at his brother. "Ok-Okay..." He whimpers slightly. "I-I can do that. I can do that." The request from his anger driven sibling began to sink in. Although this action was quite unnecessary, the request was one rooted in sadness and love.

"Are you crazy?!" Chase shouts. "Ellis you can *not* bring back that... that." He stumbles over his words unsure how to describe Ophelia anymore.

She wasn't just a girl. She had thrown the world into an eternal winter and stabbed his brother in the process. He wants to call her a monster but couldn't if he wanted to sway his siblings to his side. Once Nicholas settles down, he would be able to see that.

Chase looks over at Karmin and Casey. Karmin shakes her head, and Casey stares out the window. "Nicholas listen to me. Bringing her back would only be dangerous and you know that. You aren't thinking clearly, you're letting your emotions drive you." He takes a small step closer to the wild-eyed boy. "You're just upset because you let your guard down, felt weak and betrayed."

Nicholas couldn't hear Chase over the sound of his own heavy breathing. He keeps a hold of Ellis's collar not wanting to let go until he was sure Ellis would do what he said.

"It wasn't her fault," Casey speaks up to Chase. "It was Abigail, and she only acted that way because of Preston." He looks over at his brother. "Chase, I know you know that Preston is the bad guy here. Ophelia and Abigail were just pawns... We were just pawns."

Chase shakes his head, eyes squeezing shut. His jaw clenching, and he shook his head again.

"Not bringing back Ophelia will not change the fact that he does not care about us." He presses on.

"I don't know why," Chase mumbles after a moment. "I mean we tried so hard... *I* tried so hard, but dad was never proud." His gaze shifts to the ground. "No matter what we did." His head hangs low before he lets out a breath. "I need to go see mom," he says quietly, still shaken by what had happened to her. "She's probably scared, not knowing where we are," He mutters walking out the door.

Ellis watches his brother leave, his eyes looking back at Nicholas. "She really did love you," He watches his brother's intense eyes, his heavy breathing, the grip on his collar, on the blade. His brother was scared. He knew it well.

"She really did love you," he repeats. "She talked about you nonstop. When I first got the idea that she might've had feelings for you, I mentioned your name and her entire demeanor changed." He kept his eyes on his brother's, searching for him.

"Her eyes lit up and she started speaking so fast she started to trip over her words. She smiled *more*, which I didn't think was possible, but she did."

It was quiet again in the house besides Nicholas's breathing that had calmed down slightly during Ellis's speech.

"Of course I'll do it." Ellis repeated.

It had been a week since Nicholas dragged Ellis to where Ophelia's body lay.

It was Ellis's best kept secret that he had seen the girl's spirit in that house right behind Nicholas that night.

Phantom did his best to revive the girl. He had met her in the spirit realm where they had talked for a while. He learned that she wasn't ready to fully come back, that she believed she deserved to stay here for all the danger she caused. He tried his best to reassure her that Nicholas wasn't mad, but the best he could do was get her breathing again.

"I'm sorry I couldn't do more" He had said once Ophelia started breathing again but still lay unconscious.

Ophelia had been taken home where Thomas and his staff of specially trained doctors monitored her. Nurses would check on her every now and then, but she had one guest who rarely ever left her side.

A soft knock on the basement door revealed Karmin in the doorway. "Hey," she says softly making her way to Nicholas handing him a container of food their mother had made. "I figured you haven't eaten yet." Her eyes trail over to the girl whose color had come back, but other than that had not made much noticeable progress.

"You really did love her huh?" Karmin asks, not in an insulting way as she knew her brother was capable of love and deserving of it, but she never would have guessed that this would be the girl who brought him out of his closed off mindset. "Casey needed to speak with you. Preston is back."

This made the boy's head snap up. He cocks his head to the side but didn't say anything else.

"I'm staying to keep her company. But Casey said you wanted to know if Preston ever came back after he ran away from the consequences of his actions. We still have no whereabouts on Abigail."

Nicholas stands from his seat, his eyes looking back to Ophelia then shifted to Karmin. "You come get me the second she is awake." He disappears in his signature green light.

Chapter 23

He moves through the hallway quickly, each step landing silently despite the polished shoes that gleamed faintly under the dim overhead lights. His focus was fixed ahead, his mind already running through possible scenarios. And in all of them he came out on top.

There was no hesitation in his stride, no falter in his pace it was not the pace of someone rushing to action but the deliberate rhythm of someone who knew the world would wait for him.

He was rather patient, though excited for what lays ahead. He stopped outside Preston's office door where Casey stood. "Is he in there?" He already knew the answer.

Casey nodded and stepped aside for Nicholas to open the door.

Stepping inside, Nicholas wastes no time, his eyes landing on Preston, sitting at his desk, furiously writing in his notebook. "Finally decided to stop hiding?"

Preston doesn't look up, Rogue was not worth that much of his attention. "I did not hide from anything Rogue. I simply had more important things to handle."

"You're a coward." Nicholas spits.

"Think what you must, Rogue." He looks up. "Did you only come here to insult me? If so, you can go now."

A wicked grin spreads across his face. "Oh no. No, I'm not done yet. Growing up we were always punished for any wrongdoing." He steps aside and lets Casey in. "I think it's only fair you get the same treatment."

The old man looks at Casey and scoffs. "Him? I hope you're aware I only called him Nightmare to strike fear into our enemies, I know what he is capable of. It's not much."

"Think what you want." Nicholas shrugs. "This is payback for what you did to us growing up, to your own daughter. To Ophelia." He gives Casey a small smile before he walks out shutting the door behind him.

Casey steps forward. "This is for what you did to them, and to mother." He pauses. "Oh, you'll be happy to know that mother got her memories back... don't worry, she won't be missing you."

He steps closer, his eyes glowing faintly with a pale, haunting light. His voice was low, almost a whisper. "You've locked it away," his tone devoid of malice but full of intensity. "But it's been there, waiting."

Preston stands up, rounding the desk. "Do not make a fool of yourself, leave at once."

Slowly, Casey raises his hand, the faint glow around him intensifying. The air in the room became heavy. Preston's face twists in agony as fragments of the memory began to form.

"No! Stop!" Preston cries, dropping to his knees as the memory consumes him, each detail sharp as a blade. It was as though he was there again, unable to escape the pain. The guilt.

But Casey wasn't finished. His hand moves again, and this time, the energy around him shifts, growing darker, heavier. The light in his eyes burning brighter, and the room began to distort, the edges blurring and warping. A cold dread settles in the air as the dream took shape, a twisted reflection of Preston's deepest fears.

From the shadows, the nightmare emerged, a grotesque amalgamation of torment and terror. Its glowing eyes fixed on Preston as it advances. The sound of its movements was a sickening mix of grinding metal and distorted whispers, each one a taunting reminder of everything the old man feared most.

"No... this can't be real," Preston whispers, crawling backward, his voice trembling with terror. But the nightmare was relentless, its presence suffocating, its gaze unyielding. Casey watches with an unreadable expression, his voice calm and detached.

"You deserve a fate worse than this," he said softly, "For what you did to us, to *her*. But you being forgotten, leaving behind no legacy, no one to miss you. Is enough for me."

The nightmare lunges, its claws ripping through the fragile barrier between dream and reality. Preston screams as it engulfs him, the room erupting into chaos. The walls crack, the air filling with an otherworldly roar and then silence.

When the dust settles, Casey stands alone, the faint glow around him fading as he lowers his hand. The nightmare was gone, and so was Preston. All that remained was the faint, lingering echo of fear.

Satisfied with the screams from the other side of the door, Nicholas disappears outside the door to Ophelia's basement which swung open, and he was met with Karmin's now wide eyes. "Is everything okay?" He asks quickly.

"Yes," Karmin nods. "Yes, I was just stepping out to call you, she's awake. She only wants to see you.

Nicholas nods, "Thank you, Karmin." He walks past her, pushing open the door, his eyes immediately looking at his Ophelia. She sat up in bed staring at nothing in particular. Her color had come back but all Nicholas could focus on was the sound of her breathing, and her blue grey eyes being open. He never thought he could miss a color so much.

Her eyes caught his and she gave him a weak smile. "Nicky," She starts, her voice hoarse. "Before you yell at me just know... I would rather you didn't. I'll take a hug though."

Nicholas couldn't help but laugh as he made his way over to her. He gently hugs her, his hand moving to the back of her head as he held her. "What were you thinking?" He whispers softly.

"I was the weapon, I didn't see another way," she mumbles quietly.

"There is always some other way, I could've found one if you just—" He pauses before dropping it. "Ellis said you didn't want to fully come back here, why?" He pulls away looking in her eyes.

Ophelia hesitates, her eyes shifting between his green ones and the wall behind him. "I thought there was something rotten in me." She starts, now keeping her eyes on his. "I needed to stay behind to find it, to rid myself of it."

"My sweet Ophelia." His voice barely above a whisper. "There is nothing rotten in you. Ophelia Aldane, you are my dream and I'll be damned if I let the world convince you that you're a nightmare." He rests his hand on the side of her face. "Hell, you've changed me for the better... but only for you, everyone else is too moronic for me to remain nice." He couldn't help but smile.

Ophelia chuckles softly and nods a bit. "I didn't like being told that I was destined for something dangerous, I just wanted to choose my own future."

He moves his hand down to hers, her hand cold against his warm skin. "You can, and I'd like to be there to see whatever you choose."

The corners of his mouth lightly lift into a grin, causing the dimple in his cheek to show. "Chase was right about you being a weakness to me." He reminds her. The familiar face of confidence greets him, clinging onto it before it could leave him again.

Nicholas Peters was good at many things but confessing his true feelings to this girl he had known since childhood was not one of them. Not that he would *ever* admit that. "So, we could go at this a few ways." He hums. "Option number one, I ask you a series of trivial questions and we talk this through, keeping things strictly verbal. Or option two, we cut to the chase. Your pick."

Ophelia chuckles softly, her smile not leaving her face as he speaks. No matter the conversation he was still so himself. Before he could really finish his sentence, she leans in and kisses him gently.

Had it been anyone else that interrupted his speech he would've teleported away and demanded respect. But he accepted defeat, a rare move for him. His heart hammered in his chest, and he wondered if she could feel it.

The boy only pulls away to catch his breath, hiding his face in the crook of her neck. Slowly, he pulls away to admire her again, his face a light pink, a smug grin tugging at his features.

"How long have you been waiting to shut me up like this?" He lay next to her, his fingers intertwining with hers. "Is this what scares you? Getting close?

Ophelia could only giggle. "Maybe. But it worked didn't it" She makes room for him and looks down at their hands. "I was scared to be rejected and lose you completely." She admits. "I would've rather had you as a friend than not at all."

"Don't think you'll have to worry about that, Ophelia," he hums lightly. "You should be more worried about how you're never going to get away from me." A smile pulls at his lips.

"Us against the world." She says confidently.

"Us against the world." He repeats.

Chapter 24

She paces frantically, her boots echoing in the empty space, her hands clenching and unclenching as though trying to hold onto something that kept slipping away. Her thirty-year-old frame was tense with energy, but her movements were jerky and uncoordinated, her panic as raw and unguarded as a child's.

"I—I did everything right!" She shouts, her voice cracking, bouncing off the hollow walls. "I trained. I planned! I... I was supposed to win!" Her pacing turned to stomping, her breaths coming in short, ragged bursts. Tears streaked her face, and she swiped at them with trembling hands, frustration bubbling over. “This wasn’t supposed to happen!”

She spun suddenly, her wild eyes darting around the empty warehouse only wanting her mother to appear, to step out of the shadows and pull her into a warm embrace.

But there was no one. Just the echo of her own voice. Her thoughts spiraling as she clutches her head as if trying to physically hold them back. "Momma didn't even remember me..." She whispered, the words barely audible. Her knees starting to buckle, sinking to the cold floor, her body shaking. "I... need her... I just wanted to win..."

"I'm all alone." She whimpers, rocking back and forth now, her arms wrapping tightly around herself. "I'm back here, and she's gone. She's gone..."

She stays there, the lost child she felt herself to be. All she wanted was her mother.

That's when she saw a flash of pale green light. Her head snaps up, and she glares at the unwanted visitor. "How did you find me... Go away!" She snaps.

Nicholas shrugs. "I have my ways. Listen, I mean you no harm." He rolls his eyes. "My girlfriend vetoed my other plan. I am here to bring you back home."

"Home?!" She snaps, was this some kind of sick joke. "I don't have a home! Mom doesn't remember me, and I can't get back to the other timeline. I'm stuck!"

Nicholas shakes his head. "We brought back Rose's memories. She's waiting for you, Abigail." He opens a portal and nods his head at it. "She's right in there, been asking for you."

The mention of her real name, spoken with no malice, shocks her to her core. Her eyes flicker between the green portal and the boy next to it. "What about father?"

"He's gone." He reassures her, giving a slow nod. "He's not going to mess with you, or anyone ever again."

Abigail stares at the portal, unable to look the boy she knew as her brother in the eyes. "He's... gone?"

He let out a slow breath like the words he was about to say were against his better judgment, against everything he was trained to be. "I understand why you acted the way you did. You weren't a bad person, just a person put into a bad situation." He pauses for a moment. "You're still our sister, Abigail. We want to start over, all of us, and have the actual family that Preston pretended to the world that we were."

He gestures to the portal, where her mother was waiting, her new life was waiting. If she chose to take it.

"I could have my mom back," she whispers softly. "I could... my mom..." Tears threatened to spill but she would not let them. Not yet.

Slowly, Abigail stands on shaky legs and walks to the portal. Taking a deep breath, she steps through.

Standing just a few feet from Abigail, she looked like she hadn't changed. Her short blonde hair was sleek, framing her face. Her eyes, and her smile still held so much warmth in them.

“My Abigail,” Rose whispers softly, tears forming in her eyes. Despite how much older she looked now, she still only saw her baby.

Bolting forward, Abigail rushes into her arms hugging her tight. She presses herself into her mother’s warm embrace, relaxing against the hand holding her head. “Momma,” she whispers softly. “I am so sorry for the mess I made.”

Rose shushes her gently, her hand petting her child’s hair gently. “It’s okay, my love,” She looks up and meets Casey’s eyes.

“The nightmare is gone.”

Rampage

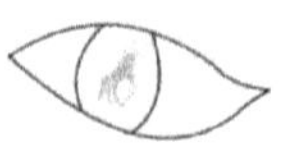

Nightmare

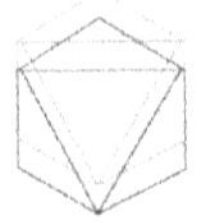

Rogue

Nexus

Phantom

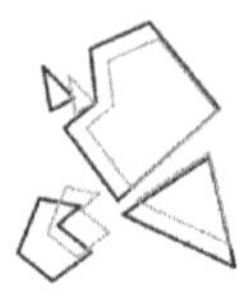

Freak

Time Bomb

www.ingramcontent.com/pod-product-compliance
Lightning Source LLC
Chambersburg PA
CBHW070637310726
48982CB00001B/310

* 9 7 9 8 2 1 8 7 4 1 6 7 9 *